❦ BOOK REVIEWS

Here's what people are saying:

Smith has cleverly blended an action-packed mystery with the problems of an independent teenager adjusting to a new family arrangement and added a colorful assortment of believable characters, both human and animal.

from SCHOOL LIBRARY JOURNAL

ESPECIALLY FOR GIRLS™
presents

A STRANGER IN THE DARK

(Original title – A Trap of Gold)

◆

ALISON SMITH

Dodd, Mead & Company

NEW YORK

Library of Congress Cataloging in Publication Data

Smith, Alison, 1932–
A trap of gold.

Summary: Thirteen-year-old Margaret finds a
mysterious, shadowy figure watching her as she searches
for a lost gold nugget from an abandoned mine.
[1. Gold mines and mining—Fiction.   2. Mystery and
detective stories]   I. Title.
PZ7.S6425Tr   1985   [Fic]   85-10427
ISBN 0-396-08721-3

To Margaret's Godmothers
Rosemary Casey and Dorothy Markinko

ACKNOWLEDGMENTS

I would like to acknowledge, with deep gratitude, the assistance of Dr. John G. Dean, of Scituate, Rhode Island, and Reno, Nevada.

I also would like to acknowledge the following reference books:

Gems and Minerals of North America by Jay Ellis Ransom, Harper & Row, 1975

The Gold Hunter's Field Book by Jay Ellis Ransom, Harper & Row, 1975

Money Mountain by Marshall Sprague, Little, Brown, 1953

The Miners, A Time-Life Book, by Robert Wallace, Time, Inc., 1976

The author wishes to thank Harper & Row, Publishers, Inc., for permission to reprint the excerpt from "Stories to Live in the World With," p. 228 from STORIES THAT COULD BE TRUE: New and Collected Poems by William Stafford. Copyright © 1971 by William Stafford.

A STRANGER
IN THE DARK

·1·

"Margaret!" It was her sister Lilian calling. "Time to do the dishes."

Margaret made a face and got up off the big old wooden swing in the backyard. For a moment, she stood there under the oak tree, thinking. It was still hot for after supper . . . ninety, maybe. The yard was still full of sunshine, except for the long, green, shady spots under the trees. But the sun was slipping down the western sky like a big dazzling ball.

Indoors, in the kitchen, it would be dark and cluttered and noisy, and even hotter. There would be greasy spaghetti pots and gluey silverware and bread crumbs everywhere. By the time she got outdoors again, the mosquitos would be out and it would be almost time to go back in again, to finish her homework and go to bed. Every night, it was the same thing.

Margaret turned away from the house. She walked to the little wooden gate in the back fence, opened it, and stepped through into the hayfield that stretched away to the banks of the Lazy River.

Behind her, she could hear the second call. "Margaret? Do you hear me? You'd better get yourself in here and do these dishes."

Lilian, again. What a nag Lilian was lately. And it was Lilian's children, mostly, who had made all that mess in there. But would Lilian ever do the dishes? Margaret snorted and kicked at a thick tuft of grass, and the trembling stalks sent a small, fluffy cloud of pollen up into the air. No, she would not. Lilian had to take care of the baby . . . or write a letter . . . or wash her hair.

Now Margaret was almost to the trees that leaned over the river, so it was even easier to pretend she didn't hear the third call.

"Margaret Cassidy! Where are you? You'd better get yourself in here, right now, you hear?"

"You'd better get yourself in here, right now," Margaret mimicked to a passing butterfly. "Because if you don't, *I* might actually have to do these dishes, myself."

And saying that, she broke into a run and raced herself to the green veil the willows dropped almost to the ground along the riverbank.

As soon as the sun slid down behind the tops of the trees on the far side of the river, the mosquitoes and fireflies came out.

Margaret loved fireflies. Her best friend, George Wilson, once told her that he had seen all the fireflies along one side of the river flash on and off in unison, for several minutes, one night. Margaret had never heard of such a thing, but she'd known George all her life and she trusted him. If he said it happened, then it happened.

Every June, after that, she sat by the river for hours in the Southern dusk, waiting for it to happen for her—but it never did.

She took out her jacknife and her matches and made a little smudge fire to keep the mosquitoes away. Not enough of a fire to be seen from the top floor of the house—just enough to fill the cool, dark spaces under the willows with drifting columns of smoke. The river made soft, contented sounds as it flowed past. It was very low, this year . . . it had been a dry spring. A whip-poorwill began calling from the Cassidy hayfield, and another "Will" answered from across the river. Margaret squatted beside her little smudge fire and sighed with contentment.

It was almost dark, now. There was just barely enough light left to write by. She pulled her diary out of a hole in the trunk of the biggest willow. She'd bought the diary this past spring . . . just about a week after her father had gone out West on the big engineering job that probably was going to keep him away all summer. It was black patent leather with a bright pink rose on the cover. She wrote in it almost every day. Tonight, she put in how much she wished Lilian would leave her alone, and how bratty Lilian's children were, and how Lilian had slapped her that morning, when their stepmother, Connie, wasn't around—and how she, Margaret, had left the dishes that evening.

When she was finished, she turned back through the pages and read bits of what she'd written in the weeks before. Darkness finally forced her to stop. She put the diary back in the willow, very carefully. Then she tossed some dry old leaves in on top of it.

A light breeze stirred the willows. The moon was rising, and soon it threw small, silvery spotlights across the damp soil under the trees. Margaret fed her little fire, and stretched out beside it. Down by the river, bullfrogs began to honk and plunk and saw, and Margaret *chur-rugg*-ed back at them. It was just about perfect, being here all by herself, with no one telling her what to do, or yelling at her. No one could get at her here. She rested her head on her arm, and fell asleep.

◆　　◆　　◆

The evening dampness and chill woke her. She was curled into a tight ball. It took her a minute or two to place herself . . . to figure out how in the world she came to be sleeping here under the willows.

She sat up. Her little fire was dying. The river, under the moon, gleamed up at her, but the space right around her was so dark she could hardly see her own hands.

Suddenly, all the bullfrogs along Margaret's stretch of river stopped honking at each other, just as if someone had pulled their switch, and Margaret knew that something was coming.

·2·

Margaret leaned forward, wondering who, or what, could have alarmed the frogs—but there was nothing moving up or down the river that she could see. Frogs! Spooky old frogs.

It was time to go home. Margaret sighed. She scooped up some damp sand and dropped it on her smudge fire. A dense cloud of smoke rose and floated out toward the river, as the fire started to smother. She bent down to get a second handful of sand and stopped, in a kneeling position. Someone *was* moving along the riverbank. She could see him now, under the branches. At least she thought it was a him. She inched forward, trying to tell if this person was someone she knew, and a small, dead stick under her knee snapped. The sound rang like a pistol shot in Margaret's ears. She froze. She didn't want to be seen out here, all by herself, this late.

Downstream, whoever it was heard the twig snap and doubled up into a deep crouch, instantly. He stayed there—absolutely still—as if he were listening, waiting for another sound.

Margaret, herself, waited impatiently for him to decide everything was all right and move on. She was so late, already. If she met one of the Cassidys' neighbors, she'd have to go through a big explanation. In River Bend, everyone just had to know everything about you . . . and if you didn't tell them, they asked.

Now whoever it was started to move again—but still in that strange half crouch. He came along the sandy shore, and then he turned in toward the willows.

Margaret drew back. Why was he coming up the bank?

For a minute she stayed where she was, absolutely quiet, hoping he would turn back down the bank and go on by, below her. But he didn't. He kept on coming. He moved purposefully, stealthily, like a cat hunting through tall grasses, looking constantly to the left and right . . . and sometimes stopping, head up, to listen.

Suddenly, Margaret realized that he *was* hunting. He was hunting her—the twig snapper! Her heart began to pound. Who could he be? What should she do? If she stayed where she was, and he kept on coming, he'd trip over her in another minute or two. If she broke and ran, and he chased her, he might catch her.

She looked around. Not far away, upstream, at the edge of the bank, a clump of shattered old willows and new willow growth leaned out in all directions from one big core. The center of the whole cluster was a deep pool of the blackest shadows. Margaret scooted through the willows into the heart of the clump and doubled up, hugging her knees.

She could actually hear him breathing, now—a hoarse, rasping sound, from the exertion of coming up over the bank bent down. She dared not raise her head to look for him in case she betrayed her position . . . or, even worse, discovered that he was looking at her.

He stopped. Margaret almost whimpered. For an unbearably long time, he stood there . . . listening. . . . Margaret didn't breathe once.

Then he started to walk again, softly, hesitantly . . . as if he were scenting the air like an animal, or studying the ground. His footsteps grew fainter. Margaret waited till she couldn't hear a sound. Only then did she dare to raise her head and look around.

She was alone. She waited another few minutes, just to be sure. Nothing moved under the willows or along the river. The bullfrogs began to *chunk* again. She climbed out of the circle of trunks and, bending very low, began to run home. When she reached the edge of the hayfield, she paused, and looked behind her—and listened. Nothing. She began to run again, racing through the grass till her legs ached and her breath was coming in short gasps. At the gate, she stopped and took one more look behind her.

The hayfield slept serenely in the moonshine. She was home, safe.

She hung over the gate for a minute, waiting to get her breath back. What would she say about this, she wondered. Nothing—that's what she'd say. Because, first of all, the man hadn't actually done anything, had he? He'd walked along the river, and then he'd come up over the bank. She couldn't prove that he had been hunting her, after he heard that twig snap. It was just one of those times when you had to have been there, to understand.

♦   ♦   ♦

She went up the steps carefully and walked along the porch to the end near the living-room window. You had to know just where to place your feet on this old flooring, if you didn't want to wake the dead. There were a couple of loose boards that creaked and squeaked like rusty hinges when you put weight on them.

She leaned over the porch railing, just far enough to peek into the living-room window. Everyone was still up. Darn! And they were all in the living room. Old Lilian was writing a letter, chewing on the eraser and frowning. By the time Margaret was twenty-five, she planned to be able to at least spell well, so she wouldn't have to copy everything three times over. Also, she planned not to have had three children.

Her brother, Bud, was studying his calculus. He was a senior in high school this year, and he was always studying calculus. It gave him a fit, but he needed it to be a geologist. Margaret had crossed geologist off her list of desirable jobs as soon as she knew that you needed calculus to be one. Even the word was ugly. C-a-l-c-u-l-u-s. It sounded like a disease or something that happened to your teeth when you got older.

Connie was looking at the television set, but she had that kind of turned-in look, and Margaret knew she was thinking, not watching.

Just as Margaret started to lean away from the window, a sound like someone playing castanets reached her through the screen, and she saw Aunt Belle come round the hall corner and flounce into the living room. Margaret groaned. Aunt Belle was Connie's aunt. She dropped in on the Cassidys now and then, in case they needed her advice. Which they didn't, Margaret thought.

Aunt Belle wore her hair piled up high on top of her head—bleached blonde, Lilian said—and she wore high,

high heels with sharp little edges that clacked along on wooden floors as if she were pounding nails. Margaret had overheard Aunt Belle tell Connie one day that she could have done a lot better in husbands than Frank Cassidy. Margaret thought that Connie could have done a lot better in aunts than Aunt Belle . . . no matter who else she picked out of the whole civilized world.

Margaret took a deep breath, opened the screen door, and went in. She said, "I'm home, Connie. Good night," and headed for the stairs.

Connie stood up. "Margaret! Thank goodness. Where have you been? Are you all right?"

"I'm all right."

"Where *were* you?"

Margaret hated it, when people asked her where she'd been like that . . . as if they were expecting her to say she'd been robbing a bank or something. "I was just around. I didn't do anything or go anywhere, really."

Connie said, "But it's ten o'clock, Margaret. We've called and called. I was beginning to think something might have happened to you."

Lilian said, "I should think you'd have had some consideration for the rest of us. Particularly Connie, who was worrying herself sick, and isn't used to teenagers, anyhow."

Connie said, "Please, Lilian, I prefer to handle this myself."

Aunt Belle said, "If you ask me, Connie, what Princess Margaret Rose needs is a good . . ."

Connie cut in. "Belle!"

"I had to do the dishes," Lilian said. "All of them. And it's your job. You have absolutely no consideration, Margaret."

Bud said, "For Pete's sake, Lilian, we've been hearing

about those dishes all night. You'd think you had to clean up after the Red Army." He turned to Margaret. "Next time, shrimp, I'm going to have to do them. So there'd better not be a next time.

Connie raised her voice. "If you would all just let me handle this . . . Margaret, where were you?"

"I was down by the river, and I sat down, and I just fell asleep. That's all. I'm sorry."

Bud groaned. "Give us a break, Maggie."

Aunt Belle said, "Down by the river! At this hour of the night? Child . . . if you were mine, I know what I'd do."

Margaret said, "I *said* I was sorry. I didn't mean to fall asleep."

"You keep a civil tongue in your head, you little snip," Lilian yelled. "And we were about to send Charlie Coffey out looking for you. So there!"

Margaret stared at her. Charlie was the town police-man. "The police?"

"Yes. The police. He was here not more than an hour ago."

Bud said, "Charlie just dropped me off, Maggie. He gave me a ride back uptown. Some convict being trans-ferred from the courthouse to jail broke loose, clobbered his guard, and took off. Charlie had to go out to the State Police barracks to pick up pictures of the guy, in case he turns up around here."

"Well, he was here, wasn't he?" Lilian demanded. "We *could* have asked him to look for her."

Margaret glanced over at Connie. "May I please go up now?"

Connie shook her head. "Margaret, we can't have this. You can't just take off and stay out till all hours. Your father wouldn't like it, I'm sure. I'm going to have to ground you. Try and understand."

Aunt Belle made a disapproving sound in her throat and noisily flipped over the pages of the magazine she'd picked up.

Margaret felt anger rise in her. No one had to tell her what her own father would and wouldn't like, least of all someone who'd never even met him till a year and a half ago . . . like Connie. Margaret and her father had known each other ever since the day Margaret was born, fourteen years ago, and, after Margaret's mother died, when Margaret was five, her father had raised her and Bud and Lilian all by himself. And they'd all gotten along just fine without any help from anyone else.

But she did not say any of that to Connie. She just said, "That's O.K., Connie," because what was the use? She'd known all along she would be grounded for taking off.

As she passed Bud, she gave him an eye signal. Then she waited for him in the front hall. He followed her out there a minute or two later.

"What's up, kid?"

"There was a man on the riverbank, tonight, Bud . . . just walking along the sand. Then he came up through the trees. He didn't see me—but he acted kind of strange. Maybe it was that escaped convict."

"No, it couldn't have been Charlie's man. They're pretty sure, from what the guy said to his buddies in the jail, that he'd heading home to Georgia . . . hitching a ride on a truck, maybe, or hopping a freight train at the grade crossing." Bud gave her a worried look. "And it's a good thing, too, because Charlie says that guy is mean. Real mean. On the All Points Bulletin, they said he should be considered 'extremely dangerous.' And you shouldn't be out alone so much at night, anyway. Something could happen to you. Didn't Dad ask you to tone it down while he was gone—to give Connie a break?"

Margaret turned toward the stairs. She remembered her father's words, all right: "I'm relying on you, Margaret, to make things as easy for Connie as you can. Take care of her for me, while I'm gone, won't you?" and Margaret had nodded, thinking how nice it would have been if, instead, he'd asked Connie to take very special care of her, Margaret.

As she climbed the stairs, she could hear Aunt Belle saying, "The police will be bringing that child home, some day," and, in spite of how she felt about Aunt Belle, Margaret's stomach tightened up and a cold chill ran along her back. Then she heard Lilian going on and on about what she, Lilian, would do if Margaret where *her* child, and she slammed her bedroom door loudly, and felt much better.

◆   ◆   ◆

The moment she looked in the mirror over her bureau, she realized that her gold nugget was gone. It was a real gold nugget, about the size of a small acorn. Her father had given it to her when he left. It was cradled in loops of thin silver wire, suspended from a silver chain, and she never, ever, took it off. But it was gone now.

She looked around her room, scanning the rug frantically in case the nugget had just that moment fallen from her neck. No. She opened her door and went down the hall and down the stairs, slowly, carefully peering into corners and looking behind furniture, in case it had rolled away. No. She went back into the living room, casually—as if she were just picking up her sweatshirt to take it upstairs. She couldn't see it in the living room. Everyone there stopped talking when she walked in, so she knew they'd been talking about her again. But she was so upset, she didn't even care.

She went back upstairs, remembering the day her father had entrusted the nugget to her. He'd been heading out the door, to catch his train—and he'd stopped to pat her cheek with his hanky because, in spite of herself, she was crying. Then he'd said, "Here, honey, you keep this for me, till I get back. Connie will get you a chain for it. You wear it for me."

Lilian had said, "Don't give her that, Daddy. She's so careless, she'll lose her head one of these days. You remember how she lost that pin of mine . . . and she loses her lunch money at least once a week. Just ask her!" And he'd turned on Lilian and said, "I'd trust Margaret with anything I owned, Lilian. You leave her alone." Lilian had flushed, and shut up.

Margaret flung herself on her bed. That nugget had been found by her own great-grandfather, right out there in the Lazy River. He'd handed it down to his son, who'd handed it down to his son—who was Margaret's father. They had all worn it proudly on their watch or key chains and shown it off to everyone.

And now, she, Margaret, had lost it. How could she tell him that? What would everyone say? What could she do? She groaned out loud and punched her pillow. It didn't help.

Somewhere out in the darkness, from near the river downstream, a dog howled. It was an awfully sad sound. Margaret had heard that dog before, nights when she'd been up sick, or lying there, trying to get over a nightmare. Late . . . real late. Just howling as if its heart would break. There were always dogs out at night in River Bend, poking around hopefully—or baying and bugling on the hot trail of some small animal. But this dog seemed to stay put. And he sounded so sad.

She pulled the pillow over her head.

·3·

Margaret woke up before her alarm went off, and her first waking thought was of the nugget. She was dressed and tiptoeing downstairs in three minutes flat.

Outside the sun had not yet come up, and a thick, thick white mist hung over the hayfield and the river.

She started with the front porch, of course. If the nugget had been dropped there, it would show up against the dull gray floor. It wasn't there. Down the steps, through the yard to the fence. Nothing. She opened the gate and poked among the long wet grasses around the gateposts. Where could it be?

When she walked into the mist, it was as if she were moving through a cloud. This would have been a very special morning . . . if it hadn't been the morning after she lost the nugget.

It was easy to trace her way back across the field. The

hay was trampled down where she had run, and pointed straight toward her house. She searched her trail—she had to look fast and keep going. Breakfast would be ready soon, and they'd be calling her.

She reached the willows on the riverbank, and was about to turn over the damp ashes of her little smudge fire, looking for a glint of gold, when she stopped with her hand poised several inches above the ground. Someone had already probed the heart of her fire! There were clear indentations where someone's fingers had worked their way down through the top layers. Who? Why? To see if the ashes were still warm?

Margaret stood up. A cold, clammy sensation wrapped itself around her as if fog were blowing through the willows.

Then, she saw the footprints. There were several of them, in a spaced-out line. They led to where the willows met the hayfield, right at the point where she had come out of the trees and started running through the field toward home. One big print lay over one of her own where she'd pushed off, digging in with her toes for every bit of speed and power she could get. So whoever it was had stepped exactly where she'd stepped.

What was going on here? Why would he come back . . . searching for her again . . . so determined to find out who had seen him?

She shook herself. There was no time for standing around and wondering. The important thing now was to find her nugget. She retraced her movements after she'd seen the man coming upriver, even climbing back into the willow clump where she'd hidden and rooting around with her hands in the center of the group. When she was down to hard ground and bare root, she stood up, defeated. The nugget had just disappeared.

Suddenly she had an idea. There were clusters of whippy new shoots all around the base of these willows. If one of those skinny little shoots had caught on the wires around the nugget and pulled till the wire or chain gave way, that nugget might have gone sailing out into the darkness . . . and she'd been so scared and in such a hurry to get away, she might not even have noticed a tug like that. The wires were thin. The chain was delicate—Connie always liked delicate stuff. It could have happened that way.

Margaret scrambled out of the willows and went around them in wider and wider circles, avoiding the place where she could see that person's footprints. She stood on the edge of the bank nearest the willows and looked down into the shallow water. She didn't see her nugget, but she knew that finding it in a pebbly riverbed, with the glimmer and rippling of the water getting in the way, could take a lot of looking.

The sun was lighting the tips of the willows on the other side of the river now. The treetops glowed a clear, silvery green against the deep, blue sky. She had to go. If she didn't get back in time for breakfast, Connie or Lilian would start asking questions. The nugget must be down there in the shallows. There wasn't any other place left. She peered over the bank again, for one last look, and almost fell into the river when another thought—a more awful thought—struck her. What if that man who had come up the riverbank had seen it, glimmering on the ground in the moonlight, and picked it up? That *could* have happened, the way he was walking—crouched over. Margaret started sweating again.

Who was that man? Who would be coming upriver late of an evening? Someone tall and thin, with big feet. Someone who moved along as if he knew exactly where he was every minute, even in the darkest places under the trees. Tall, and thin, and knew the river at night . . . Margaret said it out loud, she was so pleased with herself. "Harold! Harold Munson."

Harold was a senior at the River Bend High School, but he was not a very good student, so he was repeating two subjects that Margaret was taking this year, in order to graduate with his class. Harold went frog-gigging, sometimes. She and Bud had seen him often, heading toward the river after supper with his broom-handle gig and his gunny sack. And she'd seen him going home later, with the sack full of frogs. Anyone who went around at night frog-gigging would get to know the riverbank pretty darned well. If you stumbled around a lot, you didn't go home with a sackful of frogs.

That wasn't all. Harold had discovered that lots of snakes liked frogs for dinner, too—and he'd taken up snake collecting. To Margaret's certain knowledge, Harold carried small snakes in his pockets, sometimes. In his pockets!

Well, now she knew someone who was tall and thin, had big feet, and knew where he was going on the river. Harold must have been snaking, last night. Why he came up the bank like that when he heard the branch break, or came back again, later, she did not know—but a person who carried snakes in his pockets was not a person you could figure out very easily. He was probably hoping to scare her to death—and he almost had!

Anyway, the nugget was in the shallows or in Harold Munson's pocket—probably with a snake—and it was breakfast time. She hightailed it back across the hayfield to the house, sliding into the kitchen, breathless, just as Connie started to dish out the grits.

Conversation at breakfast was mostly "Pass the milk,

please," and "Kimberly's dribbling again." Margaret did ask Bud if they'd caught the escaped convict in Georgia.

"No sign of him, yet. But when he does get there, they'll have some welcome home party for him . . . and everybody'll be in uniform."

Connie said, "Kimberly's still dribbling," and they were back to Square One.

◆　　◆　　◆

After breakfast, when Bud and Margaret were alone in the kitchen, clearing away, Margaret said, "Bud, do you think Lilian will ever get a place of her own?"

"Who knows? If she goes back with her husband, they'll get their own place, again. But if she doesn't . . ." He shrugged. "Who knows?"

" So—*is* she going to go back with her husband, do you think?"

"I don't know, Margaret," Bud said, impatiently. "Don't ask me. Ask him. He's the one who's going to have to put up with her, if she does."

Margaret waited a minute, and then she said, "I don't suppose you know when Dad's coming home, either?"

"You know as well as I do that he'll be home when the mine is operating again. This is a big break for him—getting to help reopen a big mine like that . . . and good money, too."

"I know all that. But *when* will the mine reopen?"

"The end of the summer, maybe. How many times do you have to ask?"

"I just thought you might have heard something new."

"It's too soon to have heard something new. I wish you'd quit bringing it up."

"Well," Margaret said, "I'm sorry I bothered you."

Bud stood up and grabbed his lunch bag from the counter. "Listen, Margaret, you'd better just settle down.

Dad's not going to be here for a while, and Lilian and her kids are. And there's not a thing in this world you can do about it." He pushed out through the swinging door to the dining room.

Margaret shoved her chair back so that it bounced against the wall. She picked up a ripe peach from the bowl of fruit on the table and threw it at the kitchen door, hard. The soft flesh of the peach spattered out in a red and yellow circle, and the stone skittered back across the linoleum and hit the stove.

"Well, pardon me!" Margaret said.

Then she squeezed out the kitchen sponge and started to mop up peach.

◆　　◆　　◆

Margaret put on her pink turtleneck for school—and under it, so she'd have a knobby something where the nugget should be, she wore a little pewter mouse on a chain that George Wilson had given her for her birthday. It was going to be a hot day but, if she wore a light shirt, open at the neck, someone might notice that she wasn't wearing the nugget.

Harold Munson was in Margaret's second class, American History. He always sat in the back where he thought he could talk and sleep without the teacher's noticing. After class, Margaret waited for the first surge of kids to leave their seats and then she headed back to Harold.

"Hi, Harold."

"Yuh?"

"Look—I was down on the riverbank last night, and I lost something."

"So?"

"So—I wondered if it was you, down there, last night. You sure gave me a pretty good fright, coming up the bank like that . . . if it was."

"I don't know what you're talking about."

"Oh, yes, you do, Harold. You were down there, all right. And you didn't want anyone to know. But I don't care. Really I don't. All I want is to get back what I lost."

"I wasn't down there last night, I'm telling you. And don't you say I was. And I didn't try to scare you, either. Who'd bother trying to scare *you*? You'd just better shut up and don't go around telling lies about people—or you'll be sorry." He got up, towering over her. Margaret stepped back a little.

"I just have to find what I lost," she said. "I just have to."

"Get out of my way, shrimp," he said, and shoved past her.

Margaret sat down at the next desk. She didn't know what to think about Harold now. He was so touchy about being down at the river that he could be lying. When people were touchy like that, sometimes it meant they felt guilty . . . or were afraid you might find out something. But was the something Margaret's nugget—which Harold knew now belonged to her—or was it something else? How could she ever find out? She should have buttered him up more, before she actually asked him about it. Margaret shuddered. She'd as soon butter up a worm as Harold.

The day dragged by. Margaret was so preoccupied with the missing nugget that she paid very little attention in class.

Harold and Margaret were in the same subject again last period. Harold gave Margaret a dirty look as he walked past her desk on his way to the last row. This was his homeroom. At the end of the class, he lifted the lid of his desk and dumped in all his books and papers. He never bothered to take any work home with him.

Margaret had to pass Harold's desk on her way to the

door at the back of the room, which was closer to the exit to the bus parking lot. The afternoon sun was pouring in the windows. As she went by Harold's open desk, something in there winked at her—a golden wink.

She stopped and backed up. Then she realized that Harold was watching her with a mean look on his face. She turned away quickly and hurried out of the room. But she did not keep on going down the corridor to board her bus. That little gleam of gold could be her nugget—in Harold's desk. This could be her one chance to get it back. He'd brought it to school, maybe, and now that she was asking questions, he was going to leave it at school overnight, rather than keep it on him. She ducked into the first empty classroom and hid, waiting for the noise in the corridor to die down.

It didn't take long. People didn't hang around school in the afternoon, near the end of the school year.

Margaret walked casually back down the corridor, past his homeroom. Empty . . . as far as she could see. She cruised by again, very casually. Definitely empty. "O.K.," Margaret thought. "Let's go."

Into the classroom. Fine. Over to Harold's desk. Looking good. Up with the lid. Honestly—this was so easy. You'd think they'd put padlocks on these desks. Just anyone could break into one of them and clean it out.

Margaret reached inside, shoving Harold's books out of the way, and started checking the debris in the bottom. An old, rotten apple core, sticky candy wrappers, pens, pencils, crumbs and more crumbs. Heaps of crumbs. Margaret shivered. There were probably bugs in here. She set her jaw and went on shuffling through the mess.

Something small, and hard, and heavy! Margaret pulled it out and held it up to the light. A rock. A regular old rock. She dropped it back into the desk and stuck her head behind the lid. She'd have to see what she was doing, or this could take her all summer. And there it was! A glint of gold, in the corner. Margaret's hand closed around it . . .

A superior force pulled the desk lid out of her other hand. She came up fast, indignant. "What's the—?"

Harold! Holding the lid all the way back, and staring at her with cold, snaky eyes and a pleased smirk.

"You're in big trouble, now, Margaret Cassidy," he told her. "Come on. We're going to the office," and he grabbed her by the arm.

·4·

Long before they got to the principal's office, Margaret knew that the golden object she clutched in her hand was a large, brass button . . . the kind she had seen before on a hundred navy-blue blazers. She was going to be expelled—for a brass button! Her family was going to be disgraced—and plenty mad, too—over a brass button. People would think she was crazy.

Mr. Hightower sighed. "Thank you, Harold. You may go, now. I will handle this."

Harold left, with obvious reluctance.

"Really, Margaret!" Mr. Hightower raised his hands and eyebrows. "Theft?"

"No, sir," Margaret said stoutly. "Someone took something of mine, and I thought I saw it in Harold's desk. So I was checking it out."

"A button?" Mr. Hightower inquired mildly. "You broke into Harold's desk for a button?"

"No," Margaret said. "Something sort of like a brass button."

"What, exactly?"

Margaret squirmed. "Do I *have* to tell you, Mr. Hightower?"

"No. No, you don't. We can deal with this on the basis of what actually happened. What happened was that you were going through someone else's desk. It really doesn't matter whose desk—or what you say you were after. You were doing something that gave the appearance of snooping, at best—and theft, at worst. Harold says you were curious about the contents of his desk before he left the room—which is why he went back. He was already suspicious. Tell me, is there bad blood between you two?"

"No, sir."

"He says you accused him of chasing you, down by the river, last night . . . and taking something of yours."

Margaret could feel herself blushing. If Mr. Hightower already knew, why did he ask?

As if he had read her mind—or her expression—Mr. Hightower said, "Frankly, I found the whole thing hard to believe."

She said nothing.

"All right, Margaret. I've known you for a long time. I doubt that you're a thief. Erratic and emotional, certainly. Stubborn, absolutely. But not dishonest. So, I will ask you to write, five hundred times, 'I will stay out of other people's desks.' "

"Mr. Hightower," Margaret gasped. "That's so"—she groped for the right word—"fourth grade!"

Mr. Hightower nodded. "Yes," he said, with some satisfaction. "I do believe in making the punishment fit the crime."

Margaret glared at him.

"See you tomorrow, Margaret—with five hundred samples of your penmanship. And Margaret—you do know that if anything else is discovered to be missing from Harold's desk—or if this happens again—the punishment will have to be much more severe."

"Yes, sir," Margaret said, and charged out of the office.

◆　　◆　　◆

Margaret wasted no time, when she got home, dashing down the hall and hitting the door to the kitchen straight-arm, with the palm of her right hand. "Connie, I know I'm supposed to stay in all afternoon and evening, today . . ." Her voice died away. The person turning around at the stove with a spatula in her hand wasn't Connie. It was Lilian.

"Where's Connie?" Margaret demanded.

"At the ladies' club, at the church."

"When's she getting home?"

"Before supper. That's all I know." Lilian bent down, hauled eighteen-month-old Kimberly out from under the kitchen table by one arm, and removed a ball of aluminum foil from her mouth. "And no, you cannot go out."

"Look, Lilian . . ."

"No, you look. This is me, not Connie. And you're not going to get around me. You are *not* going out."

Margaret whirled and headed back down the hall. There was no point in trying to change Lilian's mind. The only thing that might work was if she, Margaret, admitted that she lost the nugget—but she didn't want to do that until there was no chance of ever finding it again. She couldn't even appear too anxious, right now, in case Lilian started asking her a lot of questions or noticed that the nugget was missing.

◆　　◆　　◆

They were clearing away after dinner when Bud remembered. "I saw Charlie Coffey downtown this afternoon and he said that guard died."

"The one the convict beat up?" The hot water felt good on Margaret's hand, which was cramped from writing.

"Right. Is that all the pots?"

"That's all. Well, that's a shame—about the guard."

Bud nodded. "Charlie says it'll make this convict meaner than ever. Now he knows that if they ever get their hands on him, he's going to be doing time till they turn the state pen into a ballroom."

"So he's got nothing to lose."

"Right."

Margaret shivered. "I'm glad he's headed for Georgia."

She had trouble going to sleep that night. Normally, she hardly remembered laying her head down on her pillow, but tonight she tossed and turned as if she had a pain. And then that dog started again . . . started howling, mourning.

Margaret seized her pillow and bound it over her head. But nothing could really shut a sound like that out. Not that it was loud. It wasn't, really. But it was a quavering sound—a sad sound you couldn't ignore.

Finally, in desperation, she got up and went over to the window. The sky was full of low clouds. She could see some of them as they flew in front of the moon. A storm coming. Sure enough, over to the northwest, she saw heat lightning blink on and off like a flash camera aimed at the sky. Again. And again.

Margaret sighed. Well, a thunderstorm would clear the air—sweep away this sultry feeling. She felt as if she could howl right along with that poor old dog.

She leaned on the windowsill, on her elbows, and

waited. When the rain started, and it got cool, she'd go back to bed.

There was a lull in the heat lightning . . . a time when the sky was dark and solid and silent as it hurried past over her head. And then, suddenly, the lightning flared again—closer, much closer—and in that half a second, Margaret, staring straight ahead at the willows outlining the Lazy River, saw a figure standing under the nearest tree, looking at the Cassidy house. Standing right where she'd left the willows, running home the night before.

She said, "Oh!" and dropped to the floor. After a minute or two she came up again, slowly, and waited for the next flash. When it finally came, it was weaker and farther away—and there was no one under that willow tree. No one.

Maybe there never had been. Lightning could play tricks on you. And she was tired. It could have been a shadow, or an optical illusion. She remembered the crack in a rock high on Tinker Mountain. In the winter months, the late afternoon sunlight made a deep shadow so like an old man leaning up against the rock that most people couldn't believe it was just a shadow, at first. The valley people called it "The Tinker"—and got a big kick out of fooling visitors with it. This figure under the willow—this was probably just like the Tinker.

She crept back to bed and crawled under the covers. Then, as she felt herself falling into sleep, she reached over and turned on the little bedside-table lamp.

It was still on when the next storm broke, early in the morning, and woke her with a tremendous crash as if the roof had fallen around her. Rain spattered against her windows. As her eyes opened, a flash of lightning painted her room an eerie, sick pink.

Margaret pulled her pillow over her head. Of all

mornings to have one of these big storms! Now she'd have to wait till afternoon to search the shallows for the nugget—and it might get carried downstream in the meantime. This sounded like a real gully-washer. It might even cover her nugget with silt, from upstream. If that happened, she would never find it. Someone else might, in a hundred years, maybe, when the river uncovered it again—but by then, she'd be dead and buried. She moaned and rolled over, with her pillow wrapped around her head.

The storm kept up all through breakfast . . . working its way up and down the river. It was maddening, Margaret thought. No real rain for months—and now, suddenly, rain, and more rain. Why couldn't it have waited just a little longer, having waited so long already?

◆　　◆　　◆

Margaret didn't really want to admit to another living soul that she had lost her nugget—but she knew she could trust George. George wasn't a talker. And he was patient. He'd keep at something forever, until he did what he'd set out to do. Margaret decided to ask George to help in her search.

She opened her campaign by describing as dramatically as possible the events of the night she lost the nugget. Then she told him about her attempt to recover it from Harold Munson's desk. "Only it was just a brass button, George. All that fuss—over a brass button. I was so sure it was Harold who scared me. You know how he goes down there to gig frogs and collect snakes." Margaret shuddered. "It would be just like him to try to scare someone into hysterics."

George nodded, gravely. "Maybe. Maybe it was Harold. Maybe it wasn't. But you ought to be more careful, anyhow. If you're going to go through someone's desk, you ought to at least make sure they don't catch you doing it. Some of the people around here—like Mr. Nichols, the vice principal, for instance—aren't too wild about you, Margaret."

"Why? What did I do?"

"Well, for one thing, you started that strike against the school milk, and left them with about two hundred little cartons of smelly cheese to get rid of."

"That milk was always warm and sour by the time we got to drink it."

"I know that, and you know that—but the teachers and principals never had to drink the milk, so they didn't know it. And how about the time they let you take that laboratory rat home, over Christmas vacation, for your science project in nutrition, and you wouldn't give him back, and your father had to go down to the school, and buy them another rat?"

"Listen, George, once I'd proved that if a rat doesn't get any Vitamin B, he gets sick, why'd they have to keep putting poor little old Chumley through all that? Couldn't they just take my word for it?"

"That's not the point. The point is, they think you're a nut. Whenever someone is making waves, they think it's going to turn out to be you."

"Are you going to help me look for my nugget or not?"

"Margaret, you aren't going to find that nugget. Be practical, will you? By now it's probably under a ton of sand or gravel—or maybe someone else really did take it."

"No. I go down a lot, and there's hardly ever anyone else around."

"It'll be a waste of time."

"But we've got time. It's the end of school." Margaret waited, tapping her foot. "Listen, George, remember

when your dog, Gray, whom you love more than anything else in the world, got lost, didn't I help you look?"

"Yes."

"And when you were so sick that time, and Michael
Feeney wanted to take over your paper route, didn't I do
it for you, so he couldn't?"

George sighed. "When do you want me?" he asked.

"About four, I think. I can't be too much in a hurry, in
case Lilian notices."

"See you at four."

Margaret said, "Thanks, George," and spun off to
catch the school bus. It was going to be all right. Once
George said he'd help, he'd stick with her until they
found that nugget or gave up . . . and Margaret never
gave up.

◆　　◆　　◆

George and Gray were on the riverbank by four. With
a deep sigh, Gray stretched out under the willows.
George and Margaret waded slowly, cautiously, into the
shallows. The water was running clear, and very cold,
and its coldness was a shock to their hot feet.

"The river's a lot wider today," Margaret said, uneasily.
"The night I lost the nugget, it was about half this size,
and it was flowing so quietly, you could hardly tell it was
moving."

"The storm did it," George said.

"Well, I know that," Margaret replied, irritably. "But
maybe we'd better go farther downstream, or deeper
into the current, because the storm changed things."

"Right."

"I sure wish this old river could talk," she said. George
just gave her a look.

◆　　◆　　◆

An hour later, Margaret's feet were numb from the ankles down—except for the soles, which smarted and stung from dozens of tiny cuts and bruises inflicted by the gravel in the riverbed. Her back and her neck and her shoulders ached. She climbed out of the water onto the bank and sat down with a groan. George came out and sat down, silently, beside her.

"I've been looking through moving water so much, everything's still moving in front of me," Margaret said.

"Yup."

"You going to be here tomorrow afternoon?"

"Yup." He stood up. "Come on, Gray," he said, and disappeared into the scrub willows. Gray sighed, got up slowly, and followed him.

Margaret hobbled home through the hayfield, swearing under her breath—words she'd heard Bud or her father use when something heavy fell on their toes or they banged a thumb.

◆　◆　◆

She went back by herself after supper, to look for the nugget. But it was hard to see the bottom of the river. The afterglow reflected on the surface, and the shimmer of the moving water confused her eyes. She gave up. Tomorrow. Instead, she dug out her diary and brought it up to date—about her encounter with the mysterious man on the riverbank, and losing the nugget, and Harold Munson, and George. By the time she'd gotten it all written down, it was so dark she had to guess where the lines on the paper were, and she could hear Lilian screeching from the house: "Margaret Cassidy—you'd better be back here in five minutes or you're grounded tomorrow."

Margaret walked in, just in time. She thought her sister looked kind of disappointed when she saw her.

"Where have you been?" Lilian demanded.

"I was down at the river, just fooling around."

"You're spending too much time at that river, if you ask me. It's not healthy. Why don't you hang around the drugstore, with all the other kids, or go to the library, or something."

"Maybe I don't want to."

"Don't you talk like that to me, Margaret, or you'll be stuck in this house for a week. The library will look good to you, after that."

Margaret went up to bed fast . . . before she got into any more trouble.

·5·

Margaret loved *every* Saturday morning because each one meant no school for two whole days, but this Saturday morning was even more special because it meant no school for two and a half months. She'd have plenty of time to look for her nugget, and she knew that, somehow, she'd find it. Maybe today. George had to work all morning at the grocery store, but she wouldn't mind looking by herself on a warm, sunny morning like this.

She lay in bed for a while, curled up in a comfortable ball, going over all the great things she would do during her summer vacation—swimming, fishing, camping, reading, and just hanging around. She and George could go down to the drugstore for chocolate shakes whenever they had the money—and she could stay up late every single night if she felt like it. Of course, she would have to find that nugget, first. Suddenly, impatient to get started, she got up and went downstairs two at a time.

Lilian met her at the foot of the steps. "Why, hello there, sleepyhead. Want some breakfast?"

Margaret paused on the bottom step. "Huh?"

"I said, 'Would you like me to fix you some breakfast?' French toast, maybe?"

Margaret said, "O.K.," but her guard was up. Lilian didn't dish up anything more difficult to make than cold cereal unless she was after something.

Lilian laid a paper plate in front of her with three pieces of slightly scorched French toast on it. While Margaret was eating, little Kimberly and her brothers, three-year-old Lionel and four-year-old Wade, sat across from her, lined up like birds on a telephone wire, and watched her chew every bite. Probably they'd had cold cereal right out of the box for breakfast, Margaret thought. Being watched like this made it hard to swallow, and, to top it off, the French toast was stony cold. Lilian stood by the sink and talked.

"You'll never guess who I saw last night. Doreen Moseley—from my class. You remember Doreen, don't you? She was the one with the long, blonde hair. She always did like you."

Margaret made a face at her plate. Doreen was a phony from the word "go." She liked everybody, until their backs were turned, and then, watch out!

Lilian charged ahead. "Anyhow, Doreen said, 'Fancy meeting you—and talk about lucky timing! Now you can come to this little party I'm having Saturday night. Everyone will be there. It'll be just like old times.' "

O.K. There it was. Margaret put her fork down and waited.

"So, I said, 'Why, Doreen, I'd just love to come to your party—really I would—and it would be so nice to see my old friends again. Goodness knows I never get to see any-one these days . . . but I have three little kids to look after now, and I just can't walk out and leave them.' "

Margaret got up and put her plate on the counter. She wasn't hungry any more. Lilian's kids swarmed over the toast like ants at a picnic.

"So, Doreen said, 'Why, Margaret would probably just adore to take care of her little niece and nephews.' "

"I don't like to baby-sit, Lilian."

"Now, Margaret, you know I can't ask Connie because the kids give her a headache, sometimes."

"Not sometimes. Every time," Margaret corrected. "And they don't listen to me, either. They just smart-mouth me, and they get out of bed constantly, and it's murder."

"Well, I'll talk to them, and I'll tell them they'll just have to obey."

Margaret took a deep breath and braced herself. "No."

Lilian stuck her jaw out and narrowed her eyes. Her voice sharpened to a whine, like a chain saw biting into heartwood. "Now just you look here, Margaret. I never get to go anywhere, or do anything, any more—and it seems to me the very least you can do is show a little kind-ness to your own sister!"

Margaret felt herself wilting. She said, "I have some-thing else to do." Kimberly was starting to chew on a paper plate that had fallen on the floor. Margaret said, "Kimberly is—"

Lilian cut in. "And what else could you possibly have to do on a Saturday night—at your age? Just tell me that!"

Margaret squirmed. "I've got things to do."

"Oh, I know what the problem is. You want to get paid. Well, all right! I'll pay you, if you're going to be that mer-cenary about it."

In spite of herself, because she knew it might sound as if she were actually considering giving in, Margaret said, "You're always saying that you'll pay me, but you never do." A large piece was missing from the paper plate, now, and Kimberly was gagging quietly. "Lilian, I think Kimberly's got something in her mouth."

"Don't you change the subject. I'm shocked. Truly I am. I'd hate to be as greedy as you are—taking money from your own sister, who's on welfare."

Margaret said, loudly, "Kimberly's choking, Lilian!"

Lilian spun about, scooped Kimberly off the floor, and expertly ran her index finger around the inside of the baby's mouth. A wad of soggy paper plate flew out. Without missing a beat, Lilian put her daughter down and continued, "It'll be real good experience for you, Margaret. Goodness knows you've got all the time in the world and nothing to do, and, if you baby-sit a lot, the kids will get used to you. You'll see."

"But I've got things planned already."

"You're a very selfish person, Margaret Cassidy."

Margaret just stood there. You couldn't reason with Lilian.

"And I believe, when I talk to her about it, that Connie will agree with me that you do need to learn to think of other people, once in a while."

Margaret walked out of the kitchen and kept on going—out the front door. She had a sinking feeling that Lilian was going to get her way. Again. Margaret had tried to stand up to Lilian before, but Lilian could just talk circles around anyone. She wore you down.

At the willows, Margaret took out her diary and devoted two whole pages to listing all the things she would really like to do during the summer. By the time she was finished, she felt much stronger and more cheerful. She didn't put Lilian's name in, even once, in case it jinxed the whole list.

She put the diary back with a sigh. Maybe Connie wouldn't give in to Lilian this time. But, if she did, Margaret made up her mind to stay away from home as much as possible. If they couldn't find her, they couldn't stick her with the three little monsters, and Lilian might actually have to hire someone else, for real money . . . or tame those kids, somehow.

◆　　◆　　◆

When George and Gray arrived at the riverbank on Saturday afternoon, George had two rusty old dishpans and two old shovels with him. He handed one of each to Margaret. He said, "We've been doing it wrong. Poking around, we could push your nugget deeper into the riverbed. Panning is how we should be looking for it."

"Panning is for new gold."

George shoveled up some gravel and sand and water—enough to cover the bottom of his dishpan—and started swirling the mixture around so that, on every swing, a little water and gravel sloshed out over the edge of the pan, back into the river. Gray stood beside George on the bank and watched the dishpan closely as if he thought this might be a new way of preparing his, Gray's, dinner. George said, "Gold is gold. Panning's how you find it in a river. You must have seen people out here sometimes, panning for gold."

Margaret dug up a spadeful of gravel, sand, and water, and dumped it into her pan. "Tourists."

"So what? Same principle, no matter who's doing it. Gold's heavier than gravel or water so it sinks to the bottom of the pan. The lighter stuff gets swished out and the gold stays in."

"It seems as if it ought to be more complicated than

this," Margaret said. "I mean—doesn't this look too easy to be the way you get real gold?" She swirled the mixture in her pan. "I never really believed you could do it this way."

Gray gave up on the dishpans and let himself down carefully on a damp, sandy place in the shade. Gray believed in taking life easy—unless there was something interesting to follow and possibly catch.

Half an hour later, as she tried to straighten up, Margaret remembered her comments about how easy panning for gold looked. The whole upper half of her body ached from filling and emptying her dishpan—and her legs ached from the cold water. It still didn't seem very complicated—but it sure wasn't easy.

George said, "Giving up?"

"No! Of course I'm not giving up. I was just looking for a better spot."

"I read that gravel bars in old rivers were good. There's a gravel bar over there."

"That's for new gold. My nugget is old gold. Who wrote this book, anyway?"

"Some old prospector."

"How come, if he was so rich, he had to write a book?"

"I didn't say he was rich, I said he was old."

Finally there came a moment when Margaret really truly could not straighten up to take a break. She had to shuffle over to the bank while looking at her toes. George followed her.

"Don't think I'm not coming back—because I am. I'll be here, tomorrow," she said.

"O.K. We'll be here, too—about one-thirty, I guess."

Margaret said, "Thanks, George."

George made an embarrassed noise in his throat and got up. He disappeared through the willow thickets.

Gray woke up, groaned, and got up and followed George.

It took Margaret twenty minutes to reach home, but when she got to the gate in the backyard fence, she straightened up and marched in to supper as erect as any West Point cadet.

She was going to have to talk to Ruby Dawson. Why hadn't she thought of Ruby before? Ruby knew when to expect the birds back in the spring—and where the best patches of wild berries were to be found. She concocted herb cures for warts and asthma and arthritis. You were always running into her, in the hills, collecting something, or studying something, or just sitting, thinking. She knew Cade County like most people knew the insides of their coat pockets. She would know about finding gold in the Lazy River, if anyone still living did.

Margaret decided she would skip out after supper and go see Ruby.

♦   ♦   ♦

The first thing Margaret noticed, when she walked into the kitchen, was that all three of the little troublemakers—Kimberly, Lionel, and Wade—were sitting in a row on the kitchen counter, watching Connie stir something on the stove. Usually, at this time of day, they were lined up in front of the TV upstairs, watching cartoon shows till their eyes bugged out.

Furthermore, the kids looked as if someone had spent some time on them. Their faces were clean, their hair had been combed, and for about the first time in three weeks they were wearing socks and shoes—and the socks matched.

"Oh, Margaret," Connie said, turning around. "Am I glad to see you! The kids have been kind of—restless— this afternoon. Would you keep an eye on them while I cook? And would you set the table? There'll be just the five of us tonight."

"I wanna set the table," Lionel announced as he slid down off the counter.

"What 'five' are you talking about?" Margaret asked, snatching Lionel by the back of his T-shirt as he headed for the silverware drawer.

"Why—us. Everybody here. I thought you knew."

"Knew what, Connie?"

"Well, Bud's going to a movie. He'll be grabbing something to eat downtown. And Lilian's going to Doreen's party."

"And I take care of the kids?"

Connie nodded. Then she asked, "Is something wrong, Margaret?"

Margaret let go of Lionel's shirt. Let him dump every piece of silverware in the house on the floor! She didn't care. She wasn't hungry any more, anyway. But Connie was looking at her, waiting for an answer. Connie looked tired. In the slanting, late afternoon light, Margaret could see lots of little lines and wrinkles on her face, under all that expensive make-up. And her shoulders were sagging, as if she was just aching to sit down and rest.

"Margaret, please, is something wrong?" Connie asked again. "Didn't Lilian talk to you about this evening? She said that she had."

Margaret sighed. There wasn't any point in stirring up another fight. Everyone would just get upset, and if Connie got too upset, she might say something to Margaret's father . . . and Margaret didn't want that. "Yes, Connie," she said. "She talked to me." She caught the silverware tray just in time, and thrust an eggbeater at Lionel as a consolation prize. "It's all right. I guess I just forgot."

"Oh. Well, I'll help you, of course, and between the two of us, I guess we can handle these little rascals."

"Connie, even Lilian can't handle these kids. Their daddy was the only one who could make them behave."

"Well, Lillian needs some time off, now and then. She's pretty tied down. The least we can do is take care of the kids for a few hours. It's *just* for a few hours."

Margaret nodded and forced herself to smile. Well, not smile, exactly. She had to settle for not frowning. Lilian had done it to her again. She just had to grin and bear it, so there wouldn't be a fuss.

♦ ♦ ♦

There was a sort of lull, after supper. The kids were so stuffed with corn fritters and syrup, their stomachs bulged. Connie said Margaret could go out for an hour, if she promised—absolutely promised—to be back in time to help wrestle them into bed. Margaret took off like a spooked cat, before Connie could change her mind.

·6·

Ruby's house was a low-ceilinged, two-room place, sitting all by itself beside a road that sort of petered out into a cow track, after it left the town behind. There was an outhouse stuck precariously on the sun-baked hillside beyond the house, and a wandering flagstone walk in front. Ruby always set out a garden in the spring, on both sides of the walk—but, by mid-June, the gardens had turned into small, square jungles of flowers, vegetables, herbs, and weeds.

Ruby was bending over a washboard set up on an old wooden table in the front yard when Margaret arrived. Her wash water was heating in a copper pot, hung over a crackling little fire. She was wearing her ankle-length gray skirt, and her blue denim shirt, with the sleeves rolled up above her bony little elbows. Her white hair was braided around her head, and she squinted in the sun, which made her look, Margaret thought, just exactly like one of those dried apple-head dolls.

"Hi, ya, kid," Ruby said, reaching for the bar of lye soap.

"It's hot, walking out here," Margaret said, and sat down on the ground. A big sycamore tree threw some shade into the yard, and Margaret gazed up through its huge, angular branches to the sky, while she waited for her heart to stop pounding. Finally, she said, "Ruby?"

"Still here," Ruby said, rubbing a denim shirt vigorously up and down the washboard.

"You know anything about gold?"

Ruby twisted the dripping, sudsy shirt into a roll and slapped it down on the table beside her. "Say—do I know anything about gold? I hope to tell you I know something about gold. What do you want to know?"

Margaret got up and walked over to her. "My father left me a real gold nugget on a chain, when he went out West. And I tried to take good care of it. I really did. But I lost it! I lost it, and I've looked everywhere and I just can't find it. So—I'm going to find him a new one in the river, Ruby. I've tried already, till my feet are all cut up and my legs just ache and, when I'm through, I can't even stand up straight."

"You been panning?"

Margaret nodded.

Ruby led Margaret round the end of the table to a bench. "Here. You sit yourself down and I'll make us some herb tea and we'll think about this thing."

"Ruby—there isn't any more gold around here, is there?"

Ruby filled an old enamel kettle from a rotting wooden bucket on the ground under the table. "Course there is. But you got to know where to look."

"How do you know where to look?"

Ruby took down the copper pot and hung the kettle on

the hook over her fire. "You've got to think like gold. You've got to stop being Ruby or Margaret for a while, and think like gold."

Margaret sighed. Ruby was going off into space again.

Ruby put her hands on her hips. "You're awful young to start putting on airs about things you don't even understand," she said. " 'Cause you don't know everything, yet." She carefully measured out some dried leaves from a Mason jar on the table into two cracked dimestore mugs, and then she poured boiling water over the leaves from the kettle. She sat down, closed her eyes, and rested her chin in her hands so she could inhale the vapor rising from her mug of herb tea. For a long time she sat there, breathing deeply. Margaret wondered if she'd fallen asleep, propped up like that, waiting for inspiration. Finally, Ruby shook herself and said, briskly, "Drink your tea before it gets cold on you."

"I don't like tea without sugar."

"You want sugar?" Ruby said, lifting a tin box from a carton under the table. "Why didn't you say so? Here— have some . . ." and she began to ladle sugar into Margaret's mug by the tablespoonful.

"That's enough!" Margartet protested.

"Well, make up your mind."

Margaret waited. Finally, Ruby said, "What was the question?"

"Where should I look for more gold?"

"Not in the Lazy River, child. We got to go to the source now. You'll have to go up Long Branch to find another nugget."

"The creek?"

"You know anyplace else called 'Long Branch'?"

"Why there?"

"Because," Ruby said, slowly, "the creek comes down

from the ridge. And *that's* where the mine was—the mine where they used to find gold."

"But that was a long time ago, Ruby."

"Now, we can do this two ways," Ruby said. "I can try to say something—and you can stop me and ask a dumb question and I can forget where I was and start all over—or you can sit there and drink your tea and listen and let me run through it just once."

There was a long silence. Finally, Margaret realized that she was supposed to answer. "Oh! I'll be quiet, Ruby."

Ruby sighed. "I know it's asking a lot, in your case." She took a deep breath. "Gold's heavy. Heavier than lead . . . did you know that? Don't answer," she added, hurriedly. "When I ask these rhetorical questions, you just let them slide right on by. Anyway—gold's heavy. It sits up there in a rock somewhere till something breaks it loose— weather, or someone picking at it. It's bound to be heavier than all the stuff around it, so when it starts moving—like down a mountain in a creek—as soon as things start to slow down, the gold goes plunk to the bottom. To the bottom of the bottom. And the bigger the piece of gold, the quicker it drops."

She paused and gulped down the rest of her tea. Then she pointed a crooked little index finger at Margaret. "Now, if you was to find a little color in a river—little bitty flakes or grains of gold—which way would you go looking for more? Never mind! You'd go upstream. Because the little flakes would have traveled further than the big flakes—and the big flakes would have traveled further than the tiny little nuggets . . . and the really good-sized stuff—that wouldn't hardly have traveled at all, unless the current of that river was really strong. And if the gold was being carried along the bottom—just rolling and bouncing along—it would find itself a quiet little spot—downstream of a boulder, maybe, or beside a bar or a ledge—and just settle there. And everything the river dropped into the quiet little spot after that would cover it up."

Ruby nodded, satisfied. "So you look for your gold where someone else found gold, like near the Sharpe mine . . . up the Long Branch. And you look for it where the branch slows down—where it widens, maybe, or goes around a bar—because when water slows down, it's going to drop what it's carrying."

"Well, my father told me they found our nugget in the Lazy River," Margaret insisted.

"I'm not saying they didn't. Could be that there was high water, for some reason or other—and that little nugget just got torn loose and carried along down Long Branch till it hit the river. And it could be that right there, where the branch runs into the river and slows down, because the river's a little wider than the branch, the water dropped your nugget. But you can't count on that happening again, child. You're going to have to go up the branch—close to where the gold used to come from. I have a feeling about a gravel bar"—she closed her eyes—"and seems to me that it's just about half a mile up the branch. That stream comes down the valley lickety split and begins to turn toward the south—toward the river—and there's this little bend where it goes around a bar coming out from the west bank. If there was anything of color coming down that branch when she was running wild, it might get itself dropped alongside of that gravel bar . . ." Her voice trailed off.

Margaret studied her. With Ruby, you never knew. Half the time, she was just putting on an act and watching you from under her eyelids. The other half the time, she was truly being herself, which was when you watched her from under your eyelids.

Margaret said, "If there's still gold in the mine, Ruby, why'd they close it?"

"The mine could be all played out, child—but that doesn't necessarily mean that they got every bit of gold that ever was around here. Gold is a queer and peculiar thing. Sometimes, it isn't where it ought to be—and sometimes it is where you thought it wasn't, any more. And it's got a fascination for human beings that ain't exactly healthy. It gets to them. Once you start with gold, it's hard to stop. I used to do a little prospecting, myself."

"You did?"

"I did. At first, I'd work at it off and on—and then, I got so I was working at it all the time—digging, picking, panning—till I couldn't sleep at night with the pain in my joints. But I'd be up again every morning, out there panning in all kinds of weather."

"Did you ever find any?"

"Of course I did. Just enough to keep me hooked. Finally, I got the pneumonia. Kept on working till I dropped. Someone found me—brought me in, or I'd have been dead. And the doctor, he says to me, 'Ruby, you go back out there prospecting and I don't want to see you in this office again. If they find you, so help me! I'll tell them to call someone else.' "

"Would he have?"

"Naw! But he was trying to tell me something, don't you see?" Ruby looked at Margaret. "There's days, yet, when I have to fight it. Go to digging in the garden, instead . . . or go fishing . . . but you know, days like that, every spadeful of dirt I turn over, I got to look. I just got to look—to see if there's any 'color' there . . . any little bitty flakes of gold. Can't help myself. It's in my blood, like the malaria. It's a sickness, child." She looked off into the distance.

After a minute, she started again. "One of the Sharpe boys went all the way out West to school about twelve years ago, to study how to get more gold out of that old mine—make it pay again, when the price of gold went high. I can't rightly recall which one it was."

"There were *two* Sharpe boys?"

"Yup. Brothers. Sam and Edward. Edward never could apply himself, though. So it must have been Sam went away to school. While he was still out there, studying, old Mr. Sharpe changed his mind and told Sam to find something else to learn—like regular business—because that mine was no good any more. Sam fought him on closing it down. Oh, my, but he was wild not to give up. But Mr. Sharpe knew his own mine. He *knew*. And everyone around here knew he was doing the right thing."

Margaret said, "I've seen the mine—all boarded up—over at Piney Creek. Where's Edward?"

"Edward died. He was so good-looking." Ruby sighed. "Tall, with fair hair. And dance! Child, he was the best dancer I ever did see. But he drowned in the branch."

"Oh, that's sad."

Ruby said, "It was a sad time for that family. First, old Mr. Sharpe died, the last year Sam was away. I always did think boarding up his mine killed him, even though he was the one said to do it. He left the house and the family interest in the bank to Sam, because Sam had all the gumption and the brains. He got everything worth saving."

"What'd Edward get?"

"Edward got the old mine and the land there abouts. Wasn't worth much, but Edward was mostly interested in having a good time, anyway. Oh, he'd go up to his property and walk around and talk about doing something with it some day, but it was all just talk. The mine was played-out—and what can you do with a rocky ridge?" She paused again, and Margaret could tell she was remembering young Edward and feeling sad.

"Anyhow," Ruby continued, "one day Edward didn't come back from his walk. They found his coat on a big rock overlooking the branch. It was in flood, then—early spring. He must have lost his balance and fallen in. Once he went down in that white water . . ." Ruby shook her head. "After a while, they just quit looking for him. Wasn't any point, any more. Lots of people are never found, after a flash flood. So, pretty quick, Mr. Sharpe was gone, Edward was gone, and the mine was boarded up—and there was just Sam left."

"That's terrible," Margaret said.

"Families go like that, sometimes—one thing right after another. Well, Sam's head of the bank, now. He's done all right for himself. I guess college did him some good. Maybe it was just as well they closed the mine before he got all caught up in it, trying to make it pay, trying to hold everything together." She frowned at Margaret. "I'm not real sure you should be spending your time trying to find yourself some gold, honey. I don't think your father would like it."

"You aren't going to tell him!"

"Of course not. I'm just saying, why don't *you* tell him? He'll forgive you for losing the nugget and you can just forget about this business."

"No."

Ruby shrugged. "I suppose I ought to wish that you don't find a single flake. I won't, though." She closed her eyes tightly for a minute, then opened them again.

"What were you doing?"

"A little thing I know about—to bring you luck."

Margaret hugged her. "Thank you, Ruby."

"Don't thank me," she muttered. "And when you find what you're looking for—you got to promise me that you'll stop. Right then. 'Cause I don't feel good about this. Not one bit."

"I promise. I promise."

Ruby got up slowly, as if moving hurt her. When Margaret looked back, as she started around the bend in the road, the soapy wet shirt was still rolled up on the table. Ruby had an old garden spade in her hands and was turning over a corner of one of the flower beds, bending down and looking closely at the soil she'd just uncovered.

Margaret felt a little chill go down her back. She turned toward the road home.

Margaret's father called about ten that night. Margaret had just gone up with the third round of glasses of water for the kids when the phone rang, so it was Connie who answered it.

As Margaret came back downstairs, some time later, Connie held out the phone. "It's your father. He wants to say hello."

It was amazing how close he sounded—across two thousand miles. Almost as if he were in the house.

"Hello, Dad. When are you coming home?"

"Hey—hold on. Not for a while yet. Don't tell me you miss me!"

A sudden wave of longing for her father caught Margaret off guard. It was so strong that she couldn't speak for a moment. Then she fought it down and said, "Boy, are you a conceited old man, Dad. Always thinking people are missing you."

He laughed—a big, powerful sound that came surging

through the telephone. "Well, Dempsey, I miss you, too."
Her father called her "Dempsey" sometimes, after one of
his favorite fighters.

"Is it going well?" Margaret asked. "The mine, I
mean."

"Yes. It's going great. How about you? How's it going
with you?"

Margaret didn't answer. She wouldn't complain, but
she couldn't lie to her father, either.

"Is Connie all right?" he asked. "She sounded kind of
tired."

"Well, she's not sick, or anything like that—but she
does get tired, sometimes, like tonight."

"Look, Margaret—do everything you can to make
things go smoothly for her, will you? For me?"

"I will, Dad."

"I'll make it up to you when I get home."

"That's O.K., Dad," Margaret said. Then she added,
"Don't worry about Connie."

"Good night, Dempsey. God bless."

"Good night, Dad."

The receiver clicked—and they were two thousand
miles apart again.

◆   ◆   ◆

Sunday morning, while it was still cool, Margaret went
down to the river. She sat under the big willow where she
stored her diary, and she put into the diary all the infuri-
ating, sickening details of Lilian's successful attempt to
make her baby-sit. She spent several lines on what a
treacherous, two-faced, lying nag Lilian was, and how
she used people and took advantage of some people's not
wanting to upset or burden other people. Finally, she
wrote about her father's phone call . . . and how he had
asked her to help Connie.

When she'd finished and put the diary back, she felt better—calmer. She walked home slowly, looking at the cumulus clouds floating by overhead, and feeling the sun baking into her back. The hayfield gave off a nice, warm smell as she passed through it, and butterflies rose and fell above the grasses all around her, like living flowers.

By the time she reached the little gate in the back-yard fence, she was humming "Oh, What a Beautiful Morning."

◆　　◆　　◆

Sunday afternoon, the heat came back. It hung over the hayfields and the river like an invisible weight.

Margaret told George what Ruby had said about Long Branch being a better bet, and about that gravel bar at the bend where the branch turned south. So they went up there and started panning along Ruby's bar. They worked in fifteen-minute snatches, resting up between times in the shade of the limp willows. Gray stretched out till he looked at least six feet long, exposing every inch of his body, including a long slab of pink tongue, to the air.

It was about four-thirty when Margaret began having trouble with dizziness whenever she straightened up. She groped her way back to the bank and sat down. "I'm going to have to stop, pretty soon."

"O.K. We got all summer."

"I can't wear turtlenecks all summer."

"You could just tell them, Margaret. Ever think of that?"

"You don't understand about that nugget. It's been in the family all these years—till I got my hands on it. So it's up to me to find it or one just like it."

George said, "It was an accident. They'd understand, if you told them."

Margaret shook her head. "Did you know I lost my

stepmother's umbrella—her favorite red one, from Japan? And I lost a rhinestone pin of Lilian's. I lose my lunch money all the time." She flung her arms out into the air as if she were about to fly. "Everything I so much as pick up is doomed to disappear."

"Margaret," George said flatly, "you take things too seriously."

"Ha!" Margaret said. "*You* can say that, George Wilson. You never lose anything."

George got up and waded back into the river. Margaret followed.

Because of her dizziness, when Margaret first saw the gleaming pebble in the bottom of her pan she thought her eyes were starting to give her trouble. She blinked several times and looked again—and it was still there—beautiful, glorious, and golden!

Margaret grabbed it, dropped her pan, and shouted, "Look, George—I found a nugget. I really did. It's gold!"

George plunged through the shallows to her side and stared down at her hand. "Is *that* your nugget?" he asked.

"No. Of course not. I didn't lose mine up here, and this is much smaller. And mine was wired."

"Are you sure it's even gold?"

"It's that same golden color, and it's heavy—oh, it's so heavy—and it came from Long Branch, didn't it?" Margaret began to jump up and down. "I've found my own nugget!" she shouted. Water sprayed in all directions.

George waited for her to calm down. Then, as she waded out and dropped onto the bank to catch her breath, he said, "You'll have to have someone who knows about gold tell you what it's worth. They call it 'appraising' or 'assaying' or something like that."

"Ruby."

"When do you want to go see her?"

"Tomorrow morning. First thing."

"O.K. See you at nine. Tomorrow. At the turnoff for Ruby's road."

"And George, if the nugget's worth anything, and I should ever sell it, I'm going to give you some of what I get . . . because you helped. You're the only one I could ask to help me. But don't let's tell anyone else just yet, O.K.? Because if I can't find my father's nugget I still have to find another one, a bigger one. I don't want anyone else to know until we find the right nugget."

George nodded. "Right. Come on, Gray," and they disappeared into the thickets.

Margaret put the tiny nugget deep in her jeans' pocket and turned toward home. She could hardly believe it! She'd actually found a little piece of gold. She skipped, and she ran, and she danced, and she jogged all the way. She wasn't tired any more, and she didn't ache at all. She felt like a million dollars. "It's funny what a little gold will do for you," Margaret thought, and grinned.

◆　◆　◆

A dozen times during the evening she almost told someone . . . Bud, or Connie—even Lilian. But something kept her from it. In the back of her mind was the nagging little thought that this might not really be gold, after all.

When Margaret and Bud were having milk in the kitchen before going upstairs, Bud said, "You feel all right?"

"Sure. Why?"

"I don't know. You look as if you're coming down with something. Feverish, sort of."

"Well, I'm not," Margaret said, and searched her mind for a safe subject to talk about, right away. "Did they ever catch that convict yet?"

"Nope. Charlie says about twenty people have said they saw him, but every time the police check out a lead, no Willie Davis."

"Is that his name, Willie Davis?"

"Yup. Old Chester Farley, down at the depot, even thought he'd seen him—that first night—but it didn't amount to anything." Bud dropped a book he was carrying and Margaret jumped.

"You sure are edgy tonight," he said.

"I am not."

"Well, don't go worrying about Willie Davis. Old Chester's alone too much, being a night watchman . . . and Charlie thinks he drinks on the job."

"I'm not worried about Willie Davis. He doesn't worry me at all," Margaret said, and left before she told all or exploded.

·7·

The town of River Bend lay a mile downstream from Margaret's house, at a spot where the river had changed its mind about where it was headed and made a wide U turn. A long time ago, one great big family had settled there to farm, right in the middle of that U, and a whole town had just grown up around them, till it filled the U and spread out into the broad valley beyond. Ruby's place was downriver of the town. It usually took Margaret about twenty minutes to walk to Ruby's—but this morning she was so excited, she left shortly after eight and had to sit at the crossroads, waiting for George, for a whole half hour.

Ruby wasn't home. Her cats were all outside—cleaning their fur and looking plump with breakfast. But Ruby was away somewhere—probably up in the hills. There was no telling when she'd get back.

"So—what do we do now?" George asked.

"We go see Mr. Sharpe at the bank."

"Why him?"

"He knows about gold. Ruby told me so."

"He's a banker."

"Trust me, George."

◆　　◆　　◆

Mr. Sharpe's office was located way at the rear of the bank. Margaret and George had to walk past the guard at the entrance (Margaret noted that he looked sleepy already and it was only ten o'clock in the morning), past a short line of bored people waiting for a teller (no one her age, or even a close friend of the family), past a make-believe gate and fence (as if a two-foot-high fence would keep a robber from robbing a bank!) and past three desks occupied by two serious-looking young men and Miss Morrissey, Mr. Sharpe's secretary. There was an elderly basset hound, all gray about the muzzle, tied up behind Miss Morrissey's desk. Sound asleep.

Miss Morrissey jumped up and said, "Why, Margaret Cassidy! What are you doing way back here?"

"I have to see Mr. Sharpe. It's really important, Miss Morrissey. This is George Wilson."

"Hello, George. You two just wait here and I'll see if he can spare you a minute."

Miss Morrissey was back almost immediately. "You can go in, but you'll have to make it snappy. He's got an appointment with the mayor in ten minutes."

"Yes, ma'am," Margaret said, and stepped forward.

Mr. Sharpe was surrounded entirely by dark wood—paneled walls and an old desk and plain, hard, wooden chairs. There were bars over his window, and a filmy layer of dust covered the pane like a thin shade. The only real light in the room came from the desk lamp. Margaret thought it was the most depressing room she had ever been in.

Miss Morrissey said, "Miss Margaret Cassidy and Mr. George Wilson to see you, sir," and walked out.

Mr. Sharpe said, "Yes?" and stood up. He was very tall and thin, and very stern looking. Margaret decided that bankers probably looked like that so you wouldn't try to take advantage of them and ask for too much money. Immediately she said, "We didn't come to borrow anything. We have something we'd like to show you."

"Oh? Well, that *is* a pleasant change."

Margaret pulled out the nugget, which was rolled up in tissue, and unwrapped it in the palm of her hand. "We'd like to know if this is real gold."

Mr. Sharpe leaned forward over Margaret's hand. The office was so quiet, Margaret could hear the ticking of an old clock in the corner. Then Mr. Sharpe straightened up. His face was really white, all of a sudden. He said, "Is this some kind of joke?"

"No, sir," she said.

"Who sent you here?" he asked. He looked so angry Margaret stepped back.

"No one," she said.

"Where did you get this?" he demanded.

"We found it up the branch," George said.

"Where on the branch?"

George shrugged. "Near a gravel bar. Just like the books say."

Mr. Sharpe took Margaret's nugget and held it under his desk lamp. "I suppose they told you it would be a good joke on Sam Sharpe. Well—you can go back and tell them Sam Sharpe said he still knows fool's gold when he sees it." He dropped the nugget into his wastepaper basket and brushed his hands together lightly, as if they were dirty.

"You mean"—Margaret's voice trembled in spite of all

her efforts to keep it steady—"you mean it's not real gold?"

"Of course it's not. Any idiot would know this is fool's gold."

"Please," Margaret said, loudly, "I still want it. May I have it back?"

He fished it out of the basket and dropped it into her hand. "Here! Take it back where you got it," he said, coldly.

Margaret said, "Thank you, Mr. Sharpe. Good-bye," and headed out of the office.

George caught up with her out on the street. "I'm sorry, Margaret. Those are the breaks."

"I was so sure this was gold, George. It looked just like my old nugget—only smaller." She stood on the bright, hot sidewalk for a minute, looking at the pebble in her hand. It gleamed back up at her in the sunshine. "I think I'll go see Ruby," she said.

"Why?"

"Because, out here, where the sun is, this still looks like gold to me—and Ruby will know."

"You heard Mr. Sharpe. He knew right away it was only fool's gold. He was plenty mad about it, too." George scuffed the sidewalk with his sneaker. "You just don't want to believe him. Who'll you ask, after Ruby?"

"Listen, George Wilson! It was so dark in there, I could have been handing him a lump of coal."

"Have it your own way. You will, anyhow."

"Right."

"I guess I'll see you tomorrow, about three, up the branch."

Margaret nodded. She was in a tearing hurry to get back to Ruby's place. She stuffed the nugget deep in her pocket and took off.

·8·

Ruby's front door was always open, in warm weather. You stood on the big stone that served as a doorstep and you called in to her, and, if she was home and cared to speak with you, she'd answer and come to the door. If she did not feel like talking, on any particular day, she would just not answer—and you would know to go away and try again another day.

On Margaret's second visit of the day, Ruby had returned, and she did answer and come to stand in the doorway. But she sounded grouchy and irritable. "Yes? What do you want now?"

"Ruby—I found something in Long Branch. I thought it was a little nugget, but Mr. Sharpe at the bank said it's only fool's gold."

"Well, he's the one went away to college. He should

know." Ruby started to turn away.

Margaret whipped out her nugget and shoved it at Ruby. "Here! You can at least look at it, please!"

Ruby took it in her hand and stepped out into the sunshine. She brought it up close to her right eye. Then, she rubbed it on her shirtsleeve and placed it between her front teeth and bit down on it.

Margaret held her breath.

Ruby took the nugget out of her mouth and peered at it one more time. Then she said, "Beginner's luck." She turned and held out the nugget to a big white cat stretched along a windowsill behind her. "Doesn't this beat all? I go out there year after year, and what do I get? Pneumonia and a coffee can full of small stuff. She goes up there, gets her feet wet a few times, and comes home with this."

Margaret's heart began to pound wildly. The white cat yawned hugely and went back to sleep.

"You mean—it *is* real gold?" Margaret whispered.

Ruby handed her the nugget. There were two tiny dents in the top of it now—about the size and shape of eyelashes—lined up to end. Teeth marks. Ruby said, "Say, don't you know anything about gold yet? Didn't you even try biting it?"

"No."

Ruby sighed.

"Why did Mr. Sharpe say it was fool's gold?" Margaret asked.

"Did he bite it?"

"No."

"Did he weigh it—or look at it in a real good light?"

"No."

"Well, just because he's a banker doesn't mean he's right all the time. He probably didn't think it could ever in this world really be gold—so he didn't treat it like gold."

"Wow!" Margaret said. "Now all I have to do is find a bigger one."

"You aren't going to find a bigger one. Don't you know how lucky you already been? And you promised me, Margaret Cassidy. You gave me your solemn promise that you'd quit once you found something. This here's something. So it's time for you to quit."

"But this isn't big enough!" Margaret wailed. "This is tiny. The bigger one is still waiting for me, up the branch. Way up."

"You're going back on your sacred word?" Ruby said. "Well, you just get on out of here. And don't you come back. Ruby doesn't run around with people she can't trust." And she turned on her heel and walked back into her house. And this time she did shut the door—with a loud slam.

Margaret walked home feeling as if she were in some sort of crazy dream. Her nugget was gold. She'd found some real gold. She could hardly believe it. But Ruby, who'd been her friend for a long time, was mad at her—so mad she'd told her to go away. And when Ruby got mad—she stayed mad forever. One minute, Margaret was so happy she felt as if she could fly—and the next minute, she felt a little like crying. Back and forth—all the way home—flying and crying.

◆　◆　◆

The minute the supper dishes were done, Margaret headed for the willows, down by the river.

It was a hot evening. The leaves on the trees drooped. Margaret felt headachey, but still she pulled out the diary and brought it up to date—finding the new nugget, her interview with Mr. Sharpe, and that final, triumphant moment when Ruby said the nugget was real gold.

She left out the bit about Ruby being so mad at her. Writing it down would make it more real, and she didn't want even to remember that part of the day.

She put the nugget in the willow, under her diary, before she headed home.

Connie made a big point, when Margaret got back to the house, of her joining the rest of the family for an evening of television-watching, all together.

"I didn't think there was anything good on, Connie."

"Well, there isn't really. But I'd like us all to sit down in one room, at one time, for an hour or so . . . you know . . . and maybe act like family. I always pictured us doing that, sometimes . . ." Her voice trailed off.

Margaret sat down.

The living room was usually cool . . . Connie closed all the windows and drew the drapes, early each day, to trap the cool, nighttime air indoors and keep the hot, daytime air out. But this evening, the room was still closed up—and, by nine, if felt like an oven, to Margaret. "Isn't it time to open the windows, Connie?"

"That's a real good idea, Margaret. It should be a lot cooler outside, now."

Lilian said, "Is she feverish? Just look at her. Her eyes are that sick-bright, and she's flushed, and her shirt is just sticking to her back."

"Do you feel all right, Margaret?" Connie asked.

"Yes. I feel fine. All the rest of you are sweating, too. I don't hear anyone talking about that."

"Maybe you'd feel better," Lilian said, sweetly, "if you didn't dress like an Eskimo. Just look at her. She's wearing that lavender turtleneck, again—and it must be over ninety."

Margaret could feel new sweat start up all over her. "I

like lavender," she said "Do you mind, Lilian? I'll just sit here by the window, where it's cooler, so you won't have to look at me."

"You sit in a draft, baby sister, sweating like you are, and you'll catch your death."

Margaret took a deep breath. The time had come to tell Lilian off. But, as she opened her mouth, she caught sight of Connie's face. It was tightened up with disappointment and anxiety. Once she started in on Lilian, Margaret knew, there'd be a scene that people all the way down to the corner would hear. And Connie would get all upset. She might even cry. Here she'd tried to set up a nice family evening—and everything had gone blooey already.

Margaret clamped down on all the anger inside her and turned away from Lilian. She looked out the open window into the quiet summer darkness.

There was a little breeze, now. It was moving the filmy curtains beside the window, and Margaret could feel it on her damp skin. But it was a hot breeze . . . not cooling. She tried to focus all her attention on the television. There was a program on about snakes. Margaret couldn't see it, herself—spending an hour learning more about snakes. As far as she was concerned, if they left her alone, she'd leave them alone—and that was the way she wanted it.

She only heard the creaking twice. The first time, she didn't really pay attention. Her head was aching, and she felt as if she were burning up. A little sound like a creak—outside on the porch—what was that to someone dying of heatstroke?

She realized what she'd heard just as it happened again . . . that rusty-hinge creaking of one of the porch floorboards.

Margaret stiffened and came to attention. Someone was out there on their porch, not ten feet from where she was sitting. She shrank back behind the gauzy curtains. A cold sweat poured out all over her. She looked around the living room. No one else had heard it. They were all watching television or doing their own thing. She stared hard at Bud, willing him to feel her looking at him. It didn't seem to have any effect.

"Bud!" she whispered.

Nothing.

"*Bud*!" He looked up, irritated. She got up and walked out into the hall, giving him a significant look as she passed his chair.

He came out a minute later. "This had better be good, kid. They're talking about cobras."

"Someone's out on the porch. I heard him."

"What was he doing?"

"How do I know? I heard the floorboards creaking."

"Oh, Maggie, come on. How do you know it was even a him—a person?"

"What else would make those boards creak? A cricket jumping up and down on them?"

Bud rubbed his chin. "Could have been a cricket. Or a bat. They squeak. Kind of. It's like radar."

"Will you listen to me?" Margaret hissed. "It was not a cricket or a bat. Are you afraid to go out and see who's there?"

"No, I'm not afraid."

"Well, let's go then."

"Well, all right." Bud grabbed the front screen-door handle and said, loudly, "We'll just go out there now and see."

Margaret said, "Why not hire a brass band, while we're at it?"

"You want to go first?" Bud demanded. "Be my guest."

Margaret said, "Oh, for Heaven's sake—no one's going to be out there now, anyway. Not unless they're dying, or something."

Bud threw the screen door open and marched out. Margaret was one step behind him. The porch was empty.

"You see?" he said, turning on her so he almost knocked her down.

"Did you expect whoever it was to hang around all night while we were arguing about him?"

"I'm going back in there and watch television and you can check out the next creaks yourself."

"I will. Don't worry, I will. Or I'll call Charlie Coffey. He'll catch them red-handed. Then maybe you'll believe me."

But she was only talking. Margaret wasn't any too sure now, herself. Had there been someone out there? What had she heard, really? One creak that was a possible—a maybe. It was over before she'd paid any attention to it. And one that was a definite. But a quiet definite. If it had been made by something as heavy as a man, wouldn't the noise have been louder? She tried to recreate the sound in her head. No good.

She walked back into the living room and sat down. But not by the window, this time. She pushed her chair back a little, so she was sitting beside a group of family portraits mounted on the wall.

There were no more noises on the porch, after that, and only the eleven o'clock news on television, so Margaret went up to bed as soon as the snake program was over. Her nugget was safe, and tomorrow she'd be hot on the trail of another one, farther up Long Branch.

◆   ◆   ◆

She was closing all the windows and pulling the drapes for Connie the next morning when she noticed the broken boxwood branch—right under the porch railing. The clean, fresh, white wood stuck out amongst all that glossy dark green like a neon sign.

Margaret walked out to the boxwood. The break was at least three feet off the ground—and the broken branch had been a good, sturdy, healthy piece of wood. Boxwood didn't break easily. Whoever—or whatever—had been out there on the porch last night must have gone over the railing fast and landed hard on that branch.

She took Bud out to see it as soon as he got up.

He studied it for a moment, yawned and stretched, and said, "A cat did it, probably."

"Oh, really? A cat? That was a cat? Well, I'd just like to see the cat that broke that branch—that's all I can say."

"That branch could have gotten broken any time, you know. It didn't have to be last night. Could have been days ago. You're always jumping to conclusions."

Margaret said, "I would have seen it!" but she felt the ground under the case she was building begin to slip away.

"No, you wouldn't. You only noticed it this morning because you heard the floor creaking last night."

"Ah, ha! You do believe me! You think there was someone out here, too."

Bud groaned and clapped a hand dramatically to his forehead. "I didn't say that!"

"Yes, you did. As good as. Anyway, if it wasn't a cat, what did break this—if it wasn't the person who made the floor creak?"

"How would I know? Things happen. Tree branches break sometimes all by themselves without any warning, don't they? You know they do. So—maybe boxwood does, too."

"I've lived here all my life and I never saw one of these boxwoods just fall apart like that before. Should we tell Connie?"

"No," he said. "Let's just keep this our little secret."

"You don't think we should tell her?"

"No. Definitely not. Not unless something else happens. I've got to go."

"Go! Don't let me stop you. Who needs you, anyway?" Margaret said, and stomped off around the side of the house.

·9·

The minute George and Gray showed up Tuesday afternoon, Margaret told George about her visit to Ruby's. "So, it really is gold," she finished up happily, "and we're going to work even farther upstream and find a bigger one."

"How much farther up?"

"I don't know. Why don't you go up that next bend, and I'll start down here and work back and forth across the branch toward you."

"I like it better when we can talk," George said. "This way, we'll have to yell."

Margaret looked up in surprise. "I did all the talking. I thought you weren't even listening, most of the time."

"I was listening."

"Oh. Well, I'll catch up with you as quick as I can." Margaret sat down to take off her sneakers. "How about this new dishpan? Connie gave it to me today. She saw the other one Saturday night on the front porch, and she said she didn't want me getting tetanus from working with a rusty old pan."

"What'd you tell her you were doing with it?" George asked.

"I said I was panning for gold as my summer project for English Composition, next fall." Margaret made a face, remembering. "Naturally Bud laughed till he turned red. I just let him laugh. No one takes me seriously at that house, anyway. No one."

"Ah, they're all right."

"A lot you know," Margaret said darkly, and bent to her panning.

"You're just missing your father," George said, as he started wading upstream.

◆   ◆   ◆

Gray visited first one and then the other, keeping one company for ten or fifteen minutes until he felt the need to go back and check up on the other. It was on his third visit to Margaret that he began to act strangely. Margaret was panning. She hadn't heard or seen anything out of the ordinary. But suddenly Gray stood up and faced the rise on the far side of the stream and growled. The fur along his spine bristled. His ears were cupped as far forward as possible, to catch every sound.

"What's the matter, Gray?" Margaret asked, looking toward the hill. "What's up, fella?"

Gray didn't even wag his stubby tail. He ignored Margaret and concentrated on whatever he was hearing or seeing. Now and then, he growled—a deep growl that sounded like distant thunder.

Finally, he sank back down, but he remained alert and

facing the hill. Fifteen minutes later, he trotted upstream to George.

It was after Gray had left her that Margaret got the feeling she was being watched. Every time she looked up, no matter how quickly, all she saw were the motionless trees and rocks of the rise. But every time she resumed panning, she got an uneasy impression of someone up there watching her, and moving closer.

Finally, she waded upstream to be with George and Gray.

"Well, it took you long enough," George said.

"Boy, you sure are grouchy today," Margaret told him.

There was an awkward silence. Then Margaret added, "I got this spooky feeling that someone was watching me. Gray felt it, too, when he was down there. Actually, he was the one who tipped me off."

George ruffled Gray's fuzzy topknot. "He sees things, sometimes. You shouldn't pay any attention to this old dog . . . should she, Gray?"

But a few minutes later, George stopped panning and stood still, looking across the rise.

"You're getting it now, too," Margaret said, "aren't you?"

"I don't know. You two probably just got me started."

"I wonder how we know—when someone's watching us?"

"Like the deer do, I guess. For self-preservation. An instinct, maybe, so no one can sneak up on us."

Margaret nodded. "Did I tell you there was someone listening to us—to my family—right outside our living-room window last night? I heard noises—and then, this morning, I found a big boxwood branch broken."

"Who'd do a fool thing like that?"

"I don't know," Margaret said. "You tell me why anyone would watch us this afternoon. The only thing either of us has got that's worth anything is that little nugget—and only Ruby knows about that—that it's real gold."

"Ruby," George said, thoughtfully.

"Now, why would Ruby watch us? Or listen to us?" Margaret asked.

"I don't know . . . but no one ever watched you before, did they? Till last night, after Ruby knew about the nugget."

Margaret looked at him. "Do you really think? . . ." she whispered.

"I don't know," he said.

·10·

Margaret was already sitting on the bank of the branch, Wednesday, staring at the sand below her, when George and Gray arrived.

"Something wrong?" George asked, and Gray slouched over to her side and lay down, companionably.

"Yes. We've got to work harder, George. We've got to find a bigger nugget *soon*. Lilian's started in on me . . . 'How come you never wear your T-shirts, anymore?' . . . 'You'll get a rash if you don't stop wearing all that hot clothing in hot weather.' I think she knows something's going on. I'm even locking my bedroom door, at night, in case she sneaks in to see if I'm wearing turtlenecks or sweat shirts to bed. It would be just like her—to do that."

"Are you?"

"Darned right I am. What if there was a fire, or something? Would I have time to change, with my bedroom burning up?" Margaret threw a flat stone out across the branch. It didn't skip . . . just plunked into the water like a lead weight. She said, "I'd like to go farther upstream today. There are lots more gravel bars up there."

"Well, all right—but remember—the only gold we've found, so far, is that little nugget we picked up downstream of here. And you were real lucky to find that, if you ask me."

"You see? That's the problem. You're still thinking 'little.' Think 'big,' George."

♦   ♦   ♦

For the next half hour or so, they tramped doggedly up the branch. It was wilder-looking territory, Margaret thought. They could start panning again soon. They rounded a bend in the stream and walked into a line of cattle fencing. It came down off the ridge on their left, swung across the branch, just above water level, and swooped back up the ridge on their right.

Margaret said, "Someone's blocked the river!"

George examined the fence closely. "Looks brand new. The ink on this price tag hasn't even run or faded yet."

"Well, they can't do that! We've got a right to march straight up the middle of this river any time we darn well feel like it."

"Don't take a spell, Margaret. Someone probably put it up to keep their cows from straying too far. You know how cows come down to drink, sometimes, and, when it's real hot, they just stand around in the water for hours, and then, sometimes, they follow it along."

"Well, all right," Margaret said, "but it's awful wild country to run cows in." She bent over double and slipped under the bottom strand of fencing.

At the next bend in the river, George stopped on a

long, curving gravel bank. "This would be a good place, wouldn't it? It looks just like that bar Ruby told you about."

"Yes!" Margaret said, and attacked the closest bit of gravel with the spade.

The air in the valley was hot, and still. Gray stretched out in the shade on the bank and panted himself to sleep. Sweat trickled down Margaret's brow into her eyes, and through her hair, tickling her scalp unbearably. She splashed river water onto her face and arms to keep cool, but all that extra moisture just seemed to make her more sticky, and itchy, and uncomfortable.

George straightened up and studied the sky. "It's building for something," he said.

Margaret looked. Great puffy piles of cumulus clouds were floating over the ridges to their west. The tops of the clouds, mounding high up into the clear, thin air, were sunlit and white. But the bottoms, flying low over the ridges, were dark gray and purple.

"A thunderstorm, maybe," Margaret remarked, and bent down to her pan.

"They're piling up to the north, too," George said, "as high as I've ever seen them."

"So—two thunderstorms," Margaret said. "Pan."

George dug up a shovelful of gravel.

The first sign of approaching trouble was a long, low rumble, so faint they could hardly hear it over the soft bubbling and chortling of the stream at their feet.

Gray raised his head, and his ears pricked up.

George stopped panning, and waited.

Another rumble reverberated down the gorge. It seemed to Margaret that it came to them from the north. Upriver.

Gray got to his feet and whined softly.

"He hates thunderstorms," George said and walked through the shallows to the shore. He stroked Gray's head. "It's O.K., Gray. Take it easy."

Margaret kept on panning. She wanted to stop as much as anybody, but she wasn't just looking for an excuse.

There was a series of long thunder rolls from the north, and an answering clap or two, much closer, from the west. The air in the valley pressed down . . . and seemed to make breathing hard. Margaret laid her pan on the gravel bar and walked over to George and Gray. "I give up," she said. "I can hardly get my breath, any more. It's just too hot."

George nodded. The three of them stood there, silent, waiting.

Suddenly there was a splayed fork of lightning splitting the clouds over the valley, and an immediate, deafening roar. And then, as if that had been the downbeat for the rest of the performance, a drum roll of thunder in the skies to the north. The echoes from one clap had hardly died away before the next one crashed down onto the ridges. Lightning flickered and flared almost continuously over the valley upstream.

"Boy, they're really catching it up there, aren't they," Margaret said.

George nodded.

Gray was beside himself now, whimpering and pacing. George pulled him over to a place under the bank where a higher current, sometime in the past, had carved out a little shelter. Margaret crawled in beside them. When the rains came, they'd be dry, at least.

A confused little breeze swept down the valley, and the aspens on both sides of the river held up their silvery undersides.

"Rain's coming," George said.

And it was. They could actually hear it, even above the constant thunder—an advancing roar. It came sweeping around the bend like a curtain of gray glass.

Margaret was just about to say how fortunate they were to have a roof over their heads in rain like this when George jumped up, pulled Gray out of the bank by brute force, and shouted at him to move—pointing up the hill behind them. Gray went up a few feet and stopped, trembling violently, waiting for his master. Margaret yelled, "What is the matter with you? What are you doing to that poor dog?"

George reached in and grabbed her arm. "We've got to get out of here!" he yelled back, over the rain.

"You're crazy!" Margaret yanked away.

"You want to drown?" George demanded. "Look where you are. The river hollowed that out once—and we've been sitting here, listening to a roar upstream. There's going to be a flash flood coming down here like a runaway train any minute."

Margaret scrambled out of the hole and started to work her way up the bank, trying to find footholds under the scrub, and handholds in its branches. The rain was coming down so fast she could hardly see, but once she did stop and glance back. The surface of the water looked to be at a racing boil.

"Get on up here!" George yelled, from above.

"I'm getting," Margaret panted. She was maybe ten feet above the edge of the branch, now, hanging on for dear life to what she hoped was *not* poison ivy. These banks were so much steeper, under all this green stuff, than they appeared. Gray was just burrowing through it. He was lucky.

Over to her left, Margaret noticed several large, flat

stones, set into the hillside so they almost formed a series of steps. She thrust herself through the intervening brush and came to rest, gratefully, on one of them. Clear, firm footing, at last.

"Over here!" she shouted at George.

The rock slabs went up another ten feet—"Which ought to be enough," Margaret thought, "even in a bad flash flood."

She sat down on the top rock, exhausted, leaned back to rest—and fell through a curtain of honeysuckle and Virginia creeper into dark space.

·11·

Margaret came to rest, flat on her back, on a dirt floor. She lay there a minute, trying to figure out what had happened. She was staring up at solid earth, and the dangling threads of old tree roots, and stones. She was in a cave.

She looked around in the dim green light. It was a cave, all right, but it looked as though it had been dug out of the ridge. Why would anyone dig a cave there?

A moment later, George parted the vines and let himself down beside her. "Now this is safe!" he said. "I think. We can wait it out here."

Gray dropped at George's feet, panting and trembling.

It was restful, lying there on her back, but boring. After a few moments, Margaret sat up. "Boy," she said, "for a minute there, I was really scared."

George didn't answer. He was looking out the opening in the front of the cave.

Margaret said, a little louder, "I couldn't figure out what was happening—when I fell in here."

"Want to see something?" George asked, over his shoulder.

Margaret crawled over to him and made a little peephole for herself through the vines, and took a look.

The gravel bar, and her pan, had disappeared. The calm, shallow branch of fifteen minutes ago was a muddy torrent now, leaping and foaming its way down the narrow valley. It clawed at the banks that restrained it and bit off chunks of earth and scrub like a hungry monster. While Margaret watched, it cut away the last bit of bank supporting an old dead tree, upriver from the cave. The tree slowly toppled into the water and instantly disappeared, as if something had grabbed it. It surfaced again, well below the cave, as three ten-foot lengths of gray trunk bobbing along like bits of cork, and disappeared around the bend. The whole sequence had taken less than a minute. Margaret shivered in her wet clothes. "We could have all drowned. You saved our lives."

George grunted.

"Well, it's true. I owe you my life, that's all."

George shook his head. "When you heard it coming, and saw the river rising, you would have put two and two together. You'd have been up that bank like a cat on hot bricks."

"How high will it get?"

"I don't know. I guess that depends on how long it goes on like this, raining like crazy, upriver."

Margaret's fear returned. "I don't want it to trap us in here, George ."

"Does this cave go anywhere—back there?" he asked,

peering into the gloom at the rear of their shelter.

Margaret crawled deeper into the dark. It did seem that there was a slightly blacker area in the back that could be another cave. She moved toward it cautiously, waving her left arm in front of her to locate unseen obstacles.

"George—there's a place here where it keeps on going, like a tunnel."

George joined her. "Looks like."

"I don't think I want to go any farther," Margaret said. "You never know what might be in there already."

"O.K." As George turned toward the mouth of the cave, something metal clattered near his feet. He groped around, searching. "Hey, look at this! A big flashlight."

"Does it work?" Margaret asked.

A second later, they were staring deep into the heart of a black hole.

"Where does it go, do you think?" Margaret asked.

George just shook his head.

"I'm smaller than you, so I'll go in." She reached for the torch. "I don't mind, as long as I can see whatever's in there before it sees me."

The tunnel was only about ten feet long. It opened out into a larger tunnel—so large, Margaret could stand up in it. "Hey, George," she called back. "You've got to see this. Come on."

George looked out through the vine curtain one more time and then he and Gray joined her, squeezing through the small tunnel single file. Gray started nosing around, apparently having found a new and fascinating scent. George said, "The river's still rising, but not so fast. The rain must be slowing down."

"Never mind that. Look at this." Margaret played the light beam around them. A narrow little railroad track came toward them out of the darkness on their right, curved past them, and disappeared into darkness on their left. The tunnel here was tall enough to stand up in, and just wide enough for them to stand side by side. It had been cut out of earth and rock, and braced with timbers that were dark with age and moisture.

George whistled. "Now, I know where we are. We've come out in the old mine. The Sharpe mine. It's been closed for years—boarded up, and everything."

"But that's way over on Piney Creek, George—about half a mile from here."

"Oh, sure, it starts over there. But that's just where you go in. This has got to be part of it."

"Well," Margaret said, "if that's what it is, it isn't as closed up as you thought," and she shone the flashlight on several timbers to their left. Fairly new wood. Still light in color. Whole—with no signs of rot or gouges or insect holes. "Someone's put up some new supports."

"And left the flashlight," George said. "That sure hasn't been locked up here for ten years."

Margaret moved closer to George. "So—someone's been here."

"Right. They must have come in the way we did."

"And it wasn't someone who was supposed to be here, George, or they would have taken down the boards and walked in the front door, the Piney Creek way."

George said, "O.K. But what would someone else— who wasn't supposed to be here—be doing here?"

"Stealing something—or trying to steal something. Maybe whoever it is, is trying to work the mine!"

"No one's trying to steal any gold. This mine was all played out years ago. Why do you think they closed it? If there was still gold in this mine, Mr. Sharpe'd know it— and be out here, instead of downtown in the bank."

"Maybe it's a criminal, hiding out."

"Or maybe it's just a guy who likes to be by himself . . . or a hobo . . . someone who's broke and living off the land."

Margaret moved back toward the tunnel they'd come in by. "It could be that Willie Davis," she said, in a whisper. "And he could be here, right this minute."

George thought that over for a moment or two. Then he said, "Why don't we go back and check the flood now?"

In the cool, clear light of the lookout over the branch, Margaret began to relax. Willie Davis was in Georgia, for Heaven's sake. She said, "It's probably just someone trying to get a little gold out of Mr. Sharpe's mine without telling Mr. Sharpe."

"Well, it could be, I guess."

"So, *we'd* better tell Mr. Sharpe."

"We don't owe him anything, Margaret. Not after the way he talked to us."

"That's not the point. Listen—if I *do* find a big nugget in the branch, and then he discovers that someone's been working his mine, he might claim that we'd gotten our nugget in here. Maybe he could even make us give it back . . . when it never even came from in here. But if we go to him and tell him—before we strike it rich in the branch— that someone's been trespassing on his property, he'll know it wasn't us, because we didn't act as if we had anything to hide."

George shrugged. "If it'll make you happy, we'll go tell him."

"Tomorrow morning. First thing. Nine o'clock at the bank."

"O.K. The rain's stopped."

"We'd better go home. Where's Gray?"

"Oh, he probably picked up the scent of some rats. I heard them, while we were in here. Gray loves rats."

"How do you mean, 'loves rats'?"

"I mean, he loves to chase them and catch them."

"And then what does he do with them?"

George said, "You know. He kills them. Just one big crunch, ususally."

"Crunch?" Margaret said, feeling a little sick.

"Crunch," George said, firmly. "He'll catch up with us when he's ready."

They climbed out of the cave and hauled themselves the rest of the way up the ridge. Going back down the valley was impossible till the branch receded into its bed. Over the ridge was the long way round, but it was the only way home.

When they came in sight of Margaret's house at dusk, they were still soaking wet, they were cold, and they were worn out. Margaret felt only mildly curious as to why every light in the house was on and three or four strange cars were parked in front. "Must be company," she said, "or church people. See you in front of the bank tomorrow."

"Right," George said and trudged on down the road.

Margaret climbed the porch steps. She was probably going to get up in the morning with a sore throat.

The first person she saw, when she opened the screen door, was Lilian, who immediately clutched her chest, screamed, and passed out.

·12·

Margaret stood there in the lighted hallway staring at Lilian, who was spread-eagled on the oriental rug. Then she glanced down at herself and took a survey. Muddy, yes, and damp—well, that was to be expected on a rainy day, wasn't it?—and there were all those scratches and scrapes on her arms and legs where she'd clawed her way up the bank, but there was nothing she could see that would make a normal person, or even someone like Lilian, faint.

Connie came out of the living room and stopped dead in her tracks. She'd been crying. She raced down the hall, grabbed Margaret, and hugged her, mud and all, till Margaret had to say, tactfully, "Connie . . . Connie . . . ouch!" or lose a rib.

Connie turned her loose. "Oh, thank God! I'm so glad to see you." She pulled out a hanky and blew her nose. "I was so worried, Margaret. You are all right, aren't you?" She looked as if she might be going to hug her again.

85

Margaret stepped back and said, "I'm O.K., Connie. Really." Something weird was going on here.

Bud joined them. "Where the dickens were you, all this time?" he demanded.

"All this time? It's just dusk. I've been gone this long, lots of times."

"Not when there was a flash flood—and we knew you were at the river—and you didn't come back—and we found your pan all folded up like a Chinese fortune cookie, and we figured, maybe, you were . . . gone."

"Gone? You mean . . . dead?"

Bud nodded.

Margaret took a deep breath. "Well, I'm sorry, but I was with George—and when the storm started, he figured maybe there would be a flash flood and he made me climb the ridge."

Lilian, at their feet, moaned and stirred. They all looked down at her.

"I guess we'd better get her up and onto the sofa," Bud said, and went back down the hall to the living room. When he reappeared, he had Charlie Coffey with him, and George's mother.

George's mother grabbed Margaret by the arm. "Is George all right? Where is he? Where have you been?" She was a small woman but her grip on Margaret's arm was truly painful, and the look on her face was frightening.

Margaret pulled away from Mrs. Wilson. "George is all right. He's halfway home by now, I guess. We were up the branch—and when the storm broke, we climbed the ridge and waited for it to stop, in a cave."

Mrs. Wilson said, "You almost got him killed, didn't you? He would never have been down at that river if it hadn't been for you. He told me so. He said, 'I've got to go up the river today, with Margaret. She's looking for something.' " She almost spat out the words, and her eyes narrowed into slits.

"I'm sorry," Margaret stammered, "but everything's turned out all right, hasn't it? And it could have happened to anyone."

Bud and Charlie Coffey had slung Lilian between them and carried her into the living room, and now Charlie returned. He patted Margaret on the shoulder. "Glad you're O.K., sweetheart. Take care."

"You listen to me," Mrs. Wilson shrilled at him. "You just wait a minute. I want you to hear this. This girl is a bad influence on my son—always getting him to sneak off, keeping him down at that river till all hours." She paused for a moment, then continued with a sneer. "I know what she's after. Now, I want her to stay away from my son. You hear me?" and she leaned into Margaret's face.

Margaret took a step backward. Connie forced herself between them and faced Mrs. Wilson. Her chin was sticking out—Margaret could see that, in her profile—and she looked mad. Connie said, "I believe you owe Margaret an apology, Mrs. Wilson. And I must ask you to leave my house."

Charlie took Mrs. Wilson's arm and said, "Why don't I drive you home, ma'am, and make sure George is O.K. You want to see him right away, don't you? Bud here can follow us in your car. You're going to feel a lot better once you see George. We're all tired . . ." He had her to the screen door, and was opening it. Over his shoulder, he said, "This will all be forgotten in the morning, folks. She's pretty upset just now."

Bud followed them out, and a minute later Margaret heard two car motors start up.

Lilian came staggering out of the living room. "Well, missy—you've done it again," she said to Margaret.

Connie flared up. "You leave Margaret alone," she ordered. "She's had quite enough to contend with for one night."

Lilian blinked and shut up.

Margaret said, "Could I go upstairs and take a shower, Connie? I'm feeling kind of cold."

"Of course you may," Connie replied. "You look all done in. We'll talk tomorrow." She waved her away upstairs while she walked toward Lilian. Behind Lilian, Aunt Belle—that third car in front of the house, Margaret thought—came into the hall. "Well, all's well that ends well, I guess. I would miss the whole thing. I always pick the worst time to go to the powder room. But mercy, Connie, you've got your hands full, with Sarah Bernhardt, here"—she tilted her head briefly in Lilian's direction—"and that little imp, Margaret. I'll bet you never expected all this when you married Frank Cassidy."

Margaret, in the dark at the head of the stairs, thought how appropriate it would be if one of those big, wooden balls on top of the balustrade should just happen to come loose and conk Aunt Belle on top of her dyed-bonde head.

Connie said, "Belle, I don't want to hear another word out of you about Frank Cassidy. Or Margaret, either. Not one more word."

Aunt Belle, Lilian, and Connie eddied back into the living room, and Margaret headed for the warmth, and the sweet-scented soap, and the big, furry white towels of the bathroom. As she got out of her cold, wet, gritty clothing, she could hear Lilian, Belle, and Connie still going at it, downstairs.

·13·

Margaret woke up during the night with a start. The nugget! And her diary! If the river had come swelling up out of its banks around the willows, maybe it had taken back her new nugget and ruined her five-year diary. She waited, tortured by anxiety and impatience, until the sky was a pale, pinky gray, and then she slipped downstairs and out of the house, heading for the river.

Long before she got to the willows, she was walking through soggy, weakened hay and squelching deep into spongy earth. The river had even invaded the hayfield. Most of the willows were still standing. Only a few of the oldest and the youngest had allowed themselves to be uprooted and were lying half in the river and half out, with their root pads sticking up in the air. The willow Margaret had entrusted with her diary and nugget was still upright, but it was wearing a thin coat of smelly mud from a point several feet above ground down over its roots. Margaret sighed deeply with relief. The cavity holding the diary and nugget had been just a little too high for the river to reach.

She took out the diary and made a new entry—all about the cave and the tunnel and the mine—and about the flash flood, and the reception she'd gotten at home. Then, she put the diary back and patted the willow gently.

It was time for breakfast. Now that she knew everything on the riverbank was safe, she could eat a horse.

◆　　◆　　◆

Connie and Lilian's children were sleeping late. Lilian offered to cook something but Bud, as tactfully as possible, held out for cold cereal.

"Mrs. Wilson isn't going to let George see you any more," Bud said, over his cornflakes. "Charlie said she was calling you every name in the book, all the way home last night."

Margaret laid her spoon down. "But why? What did I ever do to her?" If she lost George—who else was there, any more?

"Because she wants to keep little George all to herself, that's why. She never got over his father's walking out on her, and it's just gotten worse and worse. Charlie says she's not responsible."

"Well, I say it's a good thing," Lilian put in. "Yes, I do. If you ask me, it's just asking for trouble—the two of them, off traipsing around all day and all night."

"No one asked you," Bud said.

"I believe I'm just going to speak to Connie and bring her up to date. She's so"—Lilian flung out her hands in exasperation—"so otherworldly. Things can happen right under her nose and she just keeps on smiling."

"What things?" Margaret demanded, standing up to face Lilian.

"You *are* growing up, for one—and it's time you started acting like it."

"You mean I ought to be more like you?" Margaret shouted. "La-di-da! . . . 'Hello, Sidney, how you do go on!' . . . 'Why, Theodore, you shouldn't say things like that!' "

Lilian advanced on Margaret. "Why, you little snip!"

Bud stepped between them. "O.K. Break it up. Everyone back to her corner."

Margaret sat down, and Lilian went over to the stove to fill her coffee cup. Bud turned to Margaret. "Look, Connie's having a hard enough time, with Dad at the other end of the country—and those three kids, and all. Can't you, just for one summer, take it easy and don't make any trouble? Can't you?"

"You mean, keep my mouth shut and do as I'm told," Margaret said.

"Well, yuh. What's wrong with that?"

"Do I do what *everyone* tells me—you—Lilian—Connie—Aunt Belle—George's mother—everyone?"

"Heck, yes. Why not? Just till Dad gets back."

"That's my whole summer. That's letting even people with dirty, nasty little minds"—Margaret peered around him at Lilian—"say whatever they want . . . just sitting there and taking it . . . even when they're wrong. You wouldn't put up with that for five minutes, and you know it. And I've *been* trying," she added, desperately. "You don't know how hard I've been trying!"

"You see," Lilian said, triumphantly, "you can't even talk with her. What we've got here, my dear brother, is an unmanageable child. And, if you ask me, I think Father should be informed."

"You inform Father and I'll . . ." Margaet hunted help-lessly for something she could use against Lilian. "I'll . . ."

"You'll what?" Lilian asked.

Instead of answering, Margaret jumped up and ran out of the kitchen.

Margaret waited outside the bank till nine-fifteen, hoping as the minutes clicked by on the clock outside the drugstore that George was just delayed . . . on his way, but held up. Maybe his bicycle had a flat tire. Maybe he'd met someone he knew. By nine-fifteen, she knew. He was not coming. His mother had stopped him.

She considered just giving up and going home, but that would mean always being afraid of Mr. Sharpe's interference if—no, she corrected herself—*when* she found her big nugget. If she waited—a few days, a week—to tell him, it would make her story harder to accept, particularly if she'd just come in with another nugget. No. It had to be today—before she found any-thing else.

Miss Morrissey was at her desk, with the basset hound asleep in the corner behind her. She said, "Hello, Marga-ret. What can I do for you today? And where's your handsome boyfriend?"

"He's not my boyfriend, Miss Morrissey," Marga-ret said, feeling her face flush. "He's just my friend. He couldn't come. May I see Mr. Sharpe for just one minute?"

Miss Morrissey glanced back over her shoulder toward Mr. Sharpe's office. "He's in a mood, today, honey."

"I've got to see him. It's real important. He'll thank me for coming. Honest."

"Well, all right. But you'll still have to wait a minute. He's on the phone—long distance."

The dog woke, got up, and ambled over to say hello to

Margaret. She scratched the top of his head. "Doesn't he get awfully bored, just lying here all day?" she asked.

"Bozo? Oh, he doesn't mind. And Mr. Sharpe takes him for a walk every single evening. A long, long walk. So he gets his exercise."

Margaret looked down at the basset, who was smelling Gray on her sneakers. He was as broad as he was long. Shaped like a pickle barrel. "This dog?" she asked. "He walks *this* dog every night?"

"Yes. Bozo used to belong to Mr. Sharpe's brother. They say he was just devoted to Edward. So when Edward died, my Mr. Sharpe took Bozo home with him. Wasn't that kind? I think that was awful kind of him."

Inside Mr. Sharpe's office, someone slammed a telephone down on its cradle. Miss Morrissey raised her eyebrows at Margaret. "Don't say I didn't warn you, honey." She went to the office door and said, "Margaret Cassidy, Mr. Sharpe. For just one minute," and Margaret shot past her, into Mr. Sharpe's office.

He looked up and Margaret thought, from his expression, he was going to order her out, so she started talking fast. "Mr. Sharpe, I was in here a few days ago . . ."

He nodded. "You brought me a piece of fool's gold," he said, coldly.

Margaret decided not to straighten him out on that right away. He was mad enough already. "My friend and I were up the branch yesterday," she said, "and when the thunderstorm started, we were looking for a place to stay dry in . . ."

"Yes, yes." He had suspicious eyes, Margaret thought. She spoke even more rapidly.

"Well, anyway, George figured that there might be a flash flood—and, of course, there was—so we waited for it to go by in a little cave, in the ridge."

Mr. Sharpe was leaning forward now, frowning. "A little cave?"

"Yes. And I found a tiny tunnel going back into the ridge from the cave. It went right into your mine, we think—and someone's been up there, Mr. Sharpe. There are new timbers holding up the walls, and a flashlight that works. And we just thought you should know—that it wasn't us."

Mr. Sharpe stood up and bent over the desk. "You were actually in my mine?" His voice was so stern, Margaret wished she'd never come. "How far in did you go?" he asked. "Where did you go—which level? Did you touch anything?"

"We went in just a little way," Margaret said. "We know you've got the front entrance all boarded up, with no-trespassing signs nailed onto everything, but someone's been sneaking around behind your back, coming in from that cave. Maybe even hiding in the mine."

"That mine has been shut down for more than ten years. It is . . . it *must* be . . . in appalling condition. It's a wonder you weren't killed. Do you understand that?" He was almost shouting now.

"We were real careful," Margaret assured him.

"That's not the point. You trespassed onto private property. You had no right to be there!"

Margaret wondered how soon she could leave—if she dared to leave right now.

Mr. Sharpe came around his desk and blocked the office doorway. "I'm going to have to take steps to see that you never go in there again. Never! No matter how we had the place boarded up, no matter how many signs we put up—if there'd been a cave-in, people would have blamed us. It would have been very bad community relations for the bank, too." He leaned out the doorway.

"Miss Morrissey. Where *is* she? Oh, good. Just the man I wanted to see. Charlie! Charlie Coffey. Would you step in here for a minute?" Margaret couldn't believe her ears! He was turning her over to the police.

"Mr. Sharpe," she said, "I was trying to help you."

He ignored her. He stepped back and let Charlie into the office.

Charlie was folding his wallet and putting it into his hip pocket. "Margaret" he said, conversationally.

"Charlie," she said, looking straight ahead and standing tall.

"This girl and her friend have been trespassing in my mine," Mr. Sharpe said. "By her own admission, she has actually been inside the mine within the last twenty-four hours. They found a small side tunnel that we had somehow neglected to board up, and they walked right in—bold as you please."

"Is that right?" Charlie asked Margaret.

Margaret could feel her face burning, but she stood perfectly still, looking straight ahead.

"Officer, parts of that mine could collapse at any time. You know that. Even a radical change in humidity and barometric pressure, such as we had last night, could be the final straw."

"Yes, sir."

"Well, what are you going to do about it?"

"I'm going to take Margaret home and have a little talk with Mrs. Cassidy," Charlie said.

"It's not that I want to seem harsh," Mr. Sharpe said, but he still sounded harsh, to Margaret. "I'd never forgive myself if that child—with her whole life ahead of her—was killed in my mine. I'd never forgive myself."

"I understand," Charlie said. "I'm sure it won't happen again. Come on, Margaret."

Margaret headed for the door. She was glad to have Charlie beside her as she left—even if he was the police.

"And Mr. Sharpe," Charlie said, "I'd board that tunnel up, if I were you. If the kids can't get in, they won't get hurt."

Mr. Sharpe nodded. "Yes, yes," he said. He sounded irritated, again.

♦   ♦   ♦

The town cruiser was parked right outside the entrance to the bank, but when Margaret stopped beside it, Charlie took her arm gently and kept on going down the sidewalk. "Why don't I just walk you home, Margaret?" he said, comfortably. "No need to take the cruiser."

"I've never been brought home by the police before, Charlie," Margaret said. She hoped she wasn't going to cry.

"I know."

Charlie knocked on the screen door and, a moment later, Lilian came fluttering down the front hall in her red Chinese kimono. "Why, hello, Charlie," she trilled.

Charlie said, "Lilian, I'd like to speak to Mrs. Cassidy, if she's home."

Lilian noticed Margaret standing off to one side of the porch. "What's *she* doing with you?" She's not under arrest, or anything, is she? What are you doing out there, Margaret?"

Margaret didn't answer.

Charlie said, "If you'd just call Mrs. Cassidy . . . I'd like a minute of her time."

Lilian didn't move an inch away from the screen door, but she did look back over her shoulder and holler, "Connie! Connie? Charlie Coffey's here to see you. And I think he's got Margaret with him." She turned back. "What'd you do now?" she demanded.

Connie came running down the stairs. "Charlie! Is anything wrong? Margaret? What's going on?"

Charlie opened the screen door and stepped in. Margaret walked in behind him.

"If we could just talk for a minute, Mrs. Cassidy," Charlie said, ". . . alone? I mean, just you and me and Margaret?"

Connie said, "You'd better see about the babies, Lilian. There's no one watching them."

Lilian gave Margaret a black look and started upstairs. Connie led the way down the hall into the living room.

As soon as she was inside the French doors, Connie turned around and said, "What's the problem, Charlie? Is Margaret in some kind of trouble?"

"Well, she is and she isn't," Charlie said. "Seems like, yesterday, she and George Wilson were up on the ridge and they trespassed into Mr. Sharpe's mine—that old gold mine off Piney Creek—and Margaret, here, was down at the bank this morning—"

"You were at the bank? I didn't even know you left the house," Connie said.

"And," Charlie continued, calmly, "Margaret told Mr. Sharpe that she'd been in the mine. He got pretty excited—thinking of cave-ins and all—and he wanted to know what I was going to do about it."

"I see," Connie said, and sat down in an armchair.

"So I told him I'd just have a word with you." Charlie turned and smiled at Margaret. "She came along quietly. Actually, she hasn't said 'Boo' since we left the bank."

Connie nodded. "Is there anything you'd like to say now?" she asked.

Margaret shook her head. She could not believe the treachery of some people. Here she'd been trying to help Mr. Sharpe, as well as be honest, and he'd called the police in on her. Charlie *was* the police—no matter how nice he was.

Charlie said, "I think Mr. Sharpe just wants to feel he's done his civic duty. So, now he's done it. And I've had my word with you—so I'll be on my way."

"Thank you, Charlie," Margaret said. It wasn't Charlie's fault—and he had understood about the cruiser.

"Yes, thank you, Charlie," Connie echoed.

After she'd showed Charlie to the door, Connie came back into the living room. "Margaret?"

"Yes?"

"You must have known that was dangerous—going into the old mine."

Margaret nodded. "We could tell the timbers were real old. But none of them were falling down."

"Didn't you think something like a cave-in could happen to you?"

Margaret shrugged. "We were really careful. We walked quietly, and we talked quietly, and we left as soon as we could. We just went into the mine to see if we could find another way out—in case the river came up into the little cave. We didn't want to get trapped."

Connie looked at her. "Why do I get the feeling I'm running headfirst into a stone wall?"

"I don't know," Margaret said. "I'm not trying to be a stone wall. Honest."

"Please stay out of the mine, Margaret."

"Don't worry. No one in her right mind would go back in there, anyway."

♦　　♦　　♦

It was almost lunchtime when the first call came. Someone phoned—but when Bud picked up the receiver, he heard a click. Then it happened twice to Lilian, and once to Connie.

"Someone's casing the joint," Lilian said dramatically. "A burglar."

"At eleven-thirty in the morning?" Bud asked.

"Well, people's houses get broken into during the day, don't they?"

"What would they steal?" he asked. "The stainless steel silverware?"

Lilian said, "Well, it could be that Willie Davis. I hear he's never been caught . . . they're still looking for him."

Bud said, "Lilian, give us a break, here. If you were Willie Davis, would you spend your time breaking into a house with seven of us in it? Willie Davis has got trouble already. He doesn't need any more."

Margaret frowned. Maybe someone was after her nugget. No—no one else knew about it, except George and Ruby. And anyway, the nugget was in the willow. Of course, a burglar might not know that. She made a conscious effort to calm down. No one was after her nugget—which wasn't even worth much, probably, anyway. However, the next time the phone rang, Margaret made sure she was the one who picked it up.

She took a deep breath. "Hello?"

There was silence, and then someone said, very softly, "Margaret—is that you?"

"Yes. Who is this? George?"

"Yes. I've been trying to get you, whenever I could use the phone—and I kept getting everyone else in your family. Listen. Something's happened. Gray must be trapped in the mine. He never came home. I have to go back in there and get him."

·14·

Lilian came sauntering back into the hall and leaned up against the stair banisters, listening.

"Right," Margaret said. "That sounds real interesting. We can work on it together."

"Are you coming with me?" George whispered, tensely.

"Of course. I have to eat—but that won't take a minute—and then I'll be on my way over to your place."

"My place? No. Don't come here! The mine."

"For Heaven's sake," Margaret snapped, "don't you think I know that?" An inspiration sparkled in her mind. "Lilian's right here—you want to talk to her?"

George hung up.

Margaret turned to Lilian, who was advancing toward the phone. "One of the boys at school—but he got shy, at the last minute, and hung up."

Lilian said, "I'm not talking to any of your weird little

friends, Margaret Cassidy. And don't you ever offer to put me on the phone again," and walked off.

Margaret ate her lunch in about five bites, standing up. Then she packed up a load of handy library books from the back entry shelf and said, "I'm going out. I'll see you all later." She had the door closed behind her before anyone could ask her any questions that she didn't want to answer.

As she stepped out onto the back porch and put the books down on the bench there, she heard a dog begin to howl. From downriver. It was her late-night, howling dog . . . howling in the middle of the day, for Heaven's sake!

She ran on.

♦   ♦   ♦

When Margaret got to the mouth of the cave, George wasn't there. It bothered her, going back in the mine right after Connie had said not to—but George had lost Gray trying to help her—and George had saved her from the flash flood—so how could she refuse to help him now?

She wondered whether she should go right on in and start calling Gray on her own or wait outside the cave. She worked out a compromise. She would sit down and wait five minutes for George—and then, she would go in. Alone.

George arrived just in time—four-and-a-half minutes.

He said, "I had to wait till my mother went shopping. She doesn't want me coming here, any more, or . . ." He stopped and let his sentence trail away.

"I know," Margaret said. "She thinks I'm a bad influence."

George nodded. He looked miserable.

"I'm not supposed to be here either," Margaret said.

"It's not you," she added, hastily. "It's going into the mine. I went to the bank this morning . . ."

George interrupted. "I *tried* to get away, but my mother wouldn't let me go. She wouldn't even let me call."

Margaret said, "Well, anyway, Mr. Sharpe got angry and—get this, George—he turned me over to Charlie Coffey."

George sat down beside her. "You're kidding!"

"It was awful."

"I never thought he'd do a thing like that."

"You can never tell with adults, George. Every one of them I know, right now, is acting strange."

George said, "It sure looks like a dull summer," and Margaret knew this was as close as he could come to saying he'd miss her.

She stood up. "Let's go find Gray."

George had brought an extra flashlight so, with Margaret using the one left inside the mine and George using his own, they were all set.

When they reached the narrow-gauge railroad tracks, Margaret whispered, "Which way was he going—the last time you saw him?"

George pointed to the tunnel to their left.

As the tunnel went deeper into the ridge, it passed through solid rock. There were no more of the supporting timbers, It was shaped like a big U turned upside down. George and Margaret tried walking side by side but they kept tripping over the tracks. Finally, Margaret decided it was easier to walk single file, and she dropped back behind George.

The darkest night she had ever been out in wasn't as dark as that tunnel. Sometimes Margaret heard tiny scurrying sounds and, in spite of herself, had to wait for a moment, to let whatever it was have a chance to get out of her way. Every so often, the light from their flashlights was reflected back at them by crystals embedded in the rock walls around them. The air was heavy and damp. It chilled Margaret so that she began to shiver. Water dropped from the ceiling and ran down the walls and collected in slippery pools on the tunnel floor.

They came to two tunnels that climbed off to their left, but both of them proved to be dead ends, so they went back and followed the tracks. The next time they came to a side tunnel it went up to their right, and it kept on going, with several side tunnels of its own on each side. All of these side tunnels were dead ends, though. There was no sign of Gray. Nothing but the sound of dripping or running water now and then.

Once Margaret thought she heard a different noise in the tunnel behind her, and her heart jumped up into her throat and started pounding. She clutched George's arm. "What was that?"

"Nothing. A rat, maybe. Take it easy."

"It didn't sound like a rat. I'm not wild about rats—but that didn't even sound like a rat."

"I thought you were so crazy about that Chumley you kept."

"Chumley," Margaret said primly, "was my personal rat. I do not know the rats in this mine. I think someone's following us."

George stopped and turned toward her, listening. "Well," he said, finally, "if they are, I hope they know the way out."

"That's not funny, George, because I'm getting confused." She looked around her. "I've been up so many dead ends, and made so many turns . . . do we go to our right or our left, here?"

"Left. Up. Let's head up there."

"O.K."

The tunnel curved slightly around a jutting rock face—and their flashlights hit rock ahead of them.

"It can't be another dead end," Margaret groaned.

"It isn't. Look—it goes back to the left here, and it's going down."

"Oh." Margaret had almost passed it before she noticed a small opening in the rock to her right. It was not too much bigger than she was, which made it easy to miss in the blackness all around them.

"George," she said. "Wait. There's still another tunnel."

He flashed his light toward it. "This isn't part of the regular system. It's too small."

"It's big enough for me, so it would have been big enough for Gray. Which way will we go?"

George shook his head. "I don't know."

"Whistle. Whistle down both tunnels."

George cupped his hands around his lips and bent down so he was actually inside the opening of the small tunnel. He gave a long, long, low whistle.

Margaret said, "I heard something! Really."

"From in there?"

"Yes. Try again."

This time, she positively knew she'd hear the kind of sound a dog would make. George looked at her and nodded.

He said, "Let's go."

It wasn't easy. The tunnel was so narrow, Margaret kept bumping into rough outcroppings of rock and skinning her elbows. In some places, it was so low she had to walk bent over. The floor of the tunnel was littered with slabs of loose rock, which Margaret knew had come from the walls or roof of the tunnel and were not a good sign.

They reached a place where the tunnel split. George took the right arm of the Y and came back almost immediately. "Another dead end."

♦   ♦   ♦

Margaret sighed. "Whistle again."

He looked at the rock over his head and the debris at his feet. Then he leaned forward and whistled again, while Margaret crossed her fingers and held her breath.

From somewhere ahead of them, up the left arm of the Y, they heard an answering sound . . . a sort of feeble bark.

George said, "That's Gray!"

"Why doesn't he just come to us? Whistle again."

George looked at her.

"Go on!"

He whistled again. Again, Gray answered, but did not come.

"Something's wrong with him," George said, and started walking up the tunnel. There were two more short side tunnels—both dead ends—and then the tunnel swerved slightly and, when they'd gone round the curve, their flashlights picked out a large, gray dog lying on his side, looking up at them and wagging his tail so it slapped, slapped, slapped on the gravel behind him.

"What's wrong with him?" Margaret asked, as she bent down to pat Gray's head.

George, kneeling beside her, said, "Look at this. He's gotten himself caught in a trap." Gray's left front paw was held in the steel jaws of a massive trap that had been anchored to the tunnel wall with a chain and a pin. There was dried, blackened blood around the teeth of the trap.

"Who would set a trap like that way back here in a mine? What would anyone catch in here? There's nothing but rats." Margaret straightened up and, as she did, her flashlight swung around and something beyond Gray sent a dazzling reflection back into her eyes. She blinked. There was an opening about two feet square, several feet above the floor of the tunnel, over Gray's head. And looking into it, to see what had shone back at her, Margaret gasped. "George!"

"Not now, Margaret. I gotta' figure out what to do about poor Gray."

"Stand up and look in here. There's a little room made all of gold."

George straighted up and aimed his flashlight through the opening. "Holy Cow!"

"It's a gold room," Margaret said. And it was. It was rounded, like the inside of a big ball, and about five feet across. Gold crystals sparkled and blazed back at them from every inch of the tiny room. There were flakes of gold heaped on the floor like confetti after a wedding. "I never saw anything like this in my whole life!" Margaret said.

And behind her, in that instant, she heard footsteps coming toward them and a man's voice saying, "So—you found my little room. I was afraid that you might."

·15·

Margaret dropped her flashlight, and it clattered on the floor and rolled up against the wall. She picked it up and turned, slowly, not wanting to. Mr. Sharpe! He stood over them with a gun in his hand. He looked like a wild man—not like a River Bend banker at all.

"I'm sorry, Mr. Sharpe," George said. "We just wanted to find Gray and take him home."

Margaret was trembling uncontrollably. "Mr. Sharpe," she said, and it was hard even to talk, her jaw was quivering so, "we won't tell anyone about your gold room, honest. Not if you don't want us to. And we won't ever come back, once we get Gray out of here."

"No!" Mr. Sharpe shouted, and small crumbs of rock from the unshored roof of the tunnel pattered down on them. "I can't trust you. You'd talk. You'd tell everyone. And then it would be all over."

"But no one can take your gold," George said. "It's still your mine, isn't it? No one's going to take gold out of your mine."

Mr. Sharpe said, "No one else must ever know about my little room. No one." He turned his light into the golden room and, for a moment, his face relaxed and he actually smiled. "It's a vug," he said. "I found it myself. I knew there had to be more gold in here somewhere. Oh, yes. And I cut through all this rock looking for it. And I found it." His eyes burned with excitement.

Margaret couldn't help herself. "Did you call it a *bug*?"

Mr. Sharpe glanced at her scornfully. "A *vug*. That's a giant geode—a cavity in a rock—lined with crystals and gold. I found it ten years ago. It was meant to be mine. But if they knew about it"—the smile vanished—"they might guess . . . and I can't let that happen. Not after all these years. You get up. Just leave the dog there . . . and do what I tell you or I'll have to shoot you right now."

"We'd better go," George said to Margaret. "We'll have to leave Gray." He bent down and, as he reached over to pat his dog, the gun in Mr. Sharpe's hand went off with a roar that made Margaret's head ring. A bullet splintered a rock beside George's head, and gritty dust and small pebbles stung into Margaret's skin. Larger pieces of the ceiling fell past her face. She looked up, half expecting to see the roof of the tunnel coming down toward her. When she glanced at Mr. Sharpe, she saw that he was looking up, too . . . and his hand, the hand holding the gun, was shaking violently.

"Don't do anything like that again," Mr. Sharpe said softly. "You must only do what I tell you to do or we could all die here, right now." He motioned them to walk past him, back down the tunnel.

Margaret whispered, "He's crazy. He's going to kill us, isn't he?" She was trying hard not to cry.

George said, "It sure sounds like it."

"What'll we do?"

"Keep thinking. Don't give up."

"No talking," Mr. Sharpe yelled. "You just keep on walking, you hear? No plotting or planning."

◆   ◆   ◆

Mr. Sharpe directed them down to an older section of the mine. Shoring had been put up to hold the tunnel open, but many of the timbers had rotted and collapsed. The ones that were still standing looked as if they could go at any minute.

"There *is* going to be a cave-in," Mr. Sharpe said. "But it's going to happen down here. And then I'll be safe forever."

"Mr. Sharpe," George said patiently, "no one can take your gold."

Mr. Sharpe laughed—a high-pitched, hysterical laugh. "Do you think that's all I'm afraid of? No. It's worse than that. Now, you two go on down there, and I'll stand over here, and I'll just put one bullet right up there—and I think that will do it." He gestured to a point back down the tunnel behind them. "Yes. You two sit right there. Remember, I've got a gun. I could shoot you right now. Remember that."

George and Margaret sat down. Margaret wondered if this was all some kind of terribly real dream—or a hallucination. It was too awful to be really happening to her and George. People didn't die when they were only thirteen or so—or at least, they didn't die very often. People died when they were old.

George said, "It's going to fall on him, too, Margaret—if that's any consolation."

Mr. Sharpe said, "I heard that, boy. But you're wrong, I'm safe over here."

"It'll still get him. I took Physics, and I know. He needs dynamite and a cap and a long fuse and a lot of space to be really sure. This looks like an old part of the mine. It's going to crumble like pie crust, if it falls at all."

"What are you doing?" Margaret whispered. "Why are you warning someone who's trying to kill us?"

George spoke into her ear. "He already has the gun, doesn't he? But he doesn't have any dynamite. I'm trying to buy time."

"No talking!" Mr. Sharpe said, urgently. "I told you— no talking."

Margaret felt herself starting to slide into crying again, and she dug the fingernails on her left hand into the soft parts of her thumb and palm, to distract herself.

For a few minutes, Mr. Sharpe stood there, thinking. Margaret noticed that his hands were still trembling. The gun was actually wavering from left to right. Mr. Sharpe didn't seem to notice. Finally, he said, "You're right. Dynamite would be better. This way," and he gestured down a side tunnel with the gun. "There are supplies down here."

As Margaret started to get up she noticed that the only timber still holding the ceiling over their heads was already cracked halfway up. She bent over and fiddled with her sneaker while she looked, out of the corners of her eyes, at that timber. It was rotten . . . and it was broken. That crack in the middle was really wide at the back, and the top of the timber was already leaning away from the side wall of the tunnel and sagging in. Maybe, if she hit that post hard enough, it might give, and when it gave . . .

She allowed her flashlight to slip in her hand and point up, and she glanced at the roof of the tunnel. Yes. There were cracks in the rock overhead. Big cracks. The timber beside her was jammed against a big slab of stone that had already pulled free from the surrounding rock at one corner. The whole thing was ready to go, when this last post went.

"Move!" Mr. Sharpe said, insistently. "Stop stalling, girl."

"My foot hurts," Margaret complained. "Something terribly sharp has gotten into my sneaker." She dared not look up at him in case he saw what she was planning in her eyes.

"George," she whined, "My foot is cut. Can't you at least give me a hand up?"

George just looked at her.

Mr. Sharpe glared at him. "Well, go on. Get her moving! Take her down there . . ." and he pointed again with his gun.

George said, "Why should we do what you tell us? You're going to kill us anyway."

Margaret reached for him and grabbed his arm and pulled him over. She took one small step—a hop, really, on her "good" foot. His ear, as he bent to help her, was close to her mouth. She whispered, "Post," and tripped and fell down at the base of the timber.

George leaned over and grabbed her arm. "Come on, Margaret."

Mr. Sharpe yelled, "Stop stalling or I'll shoot you right now. I'll do it if I have to. You know I will."

Margaret leaned against the post as she got to her feet, and she felt it tremble. It wouldn't take much. She pulled George closer and said, "Cracked," in his ear. She saw that he understood, suddenly.

Mr. Sharpe came toward them, waving his gun. "This is the last time I'm going to tell you. Go down there!" and he gestured down the tunnel.

Margaret let go of George's arm. She'd have to be free to put her whole self into this. She closed her eyes for a second. She was the most scared she'd ever been in her life. If she hit that post and it didn't give way, Mr. Sharpe would shoot her right then and there. She knew that. If she hit it and it did give way, there was no telling how much of the tunnel might cave in. Could be just a little— could be the whole thing. But this way she and George would have a chance. Mr. Sharpe's way, they'd have no chance at all. She took one last deep, deep breath.

Mr. Sharpe noticed. Noticed, and knew that she was about to try something. His eyes narrowed and he brought his gun up a little higher and began to aim it directly at her. Margaret screamed a tight little scream.

George shouted, "No!" and dove at him, and Mr. Sharpe straight-armed George and sent him flying back down the tunnel. As he steadied himself again and began to bring the gun back into line with Margaret, she yelled, "Run, George!" and took two quick steps back, then threw herself at the side of the cracked post with all her strength. Her shoulder hit it so hard that pain shot all through her. The post made a grating sound and there was a loud crack as it started to fall. Over her head, Margaret heard snapping, as if something strong was being broken. She ran shrieking into darkness as the tunnel caved in. She could hear rocks falling. A dust cloud came up behind her and passed her, filling her eyes and mouth with grit. She ran into the right side of the tunnel and banged the right side of her face and her right arm . . . but she pulled away and kept on running. The noise of what was happening behind her was deafening . . . and it echoed and reverberated through the mine. Small pieces of rock were hitting her face as she ran. They were falling from the roof overhead, and she knew she could have started a chain reaction that might eventually catch up with her, like the dust cloud . . . might eventually bring down the whole mine.

·16·

She ran until she couldn't run any more. When she stopped she could feel her heart pounding wildly in her chest. What had she done? George had tried to save her but maybe she'd killed him—or made Mr. Sharpe so mad, he'd killed him. She had to get out of this mine right away and go for help. That was the only thing she could do for George now—get out and get help.

She had to decide which way to go, first—and, while she was trying to make up her mind about that, she began to realize she might have sealed herself into a dead end. She wanted to start running again, in any direction—and keep running till she was out. Panic made it hard for her to think. Her mind was spinning like a pinwheel. So she started to talk to herself out loud, very firmly, reminding herself that the mine was like a big ant farm—and there was bound to be a way out. Her hands were shaking so she could hardly hold the flashlight. If she dropped that, and it broke . . . she grabbed the light hard with both hands.

She started walking, and at each intersection of tunnels, she chose to go downhill. As she walked, she played the light beam on the tunnel walls, trying to recognize a distinctive group of crystals or a pool of water or a familiar turnoff. Finally, as she passed a side tunnel, she picked up a faint impression that the air around her stirred . . . that it was just barely moving down that tunnel.

She backed up and stood in the opening, and forced herself to turn off her flashlight so she could concentrate. Yes. The air around her was moving, and the darkness down that tunnel seemed just a little less black than the darkness she'd come from.

She started walking, following the flow of air, and praying out loud: "Oh, Lord, please let this be the right tunnel. Please, Lord, get me out of this, and I'll never complain about anything again, as long as I live."

Another tunnel cut in from the left—and there were the familiar narrow-gauge railroad tracks running down the center of the tunnel floor. She stumbled along the tracks, growing more and more hopeful. Suddenly she rounded a slight bend and came face to face with the tiny molehole tunnel leading in from the cave on the hillside above the branch. Two minutes later, she was out in the fresh air, with blue sky overhead. She sat down on the slab of stone at the entrance and cried a little. She couldn't help it.

The thought of George and Gary still trapped in that awful blackness with Mr. Sharpe and his gun brought her to her feet in a few minutes, and she started running down the hillside, headed home.

◆　　◆　　◆

Bud was in the living room. "Take me to Charlie Coffey," Margaret begged, breathing hard. "Hurry, Bud—right now."

"What in the world happened to you?"

"Never mind that. I'll tell you on the way," she cried, and pulled at his arm. "We have to hurry. Now."

Bud let her drag him out to the car. "What do you want with Charlie? Say—that Mrs. Wilson didn't have anything to do with this, did she?"

"No. It was Mr. Sharpe."

Bud looked at her. "Mr. Sharpe? At the bank?"

"Drive!" Margaret shouted.

Bud started the car.

♦   ♦   ♦

Charlie Coffey was out. Wade Emery, a deputy listened to Margaret without interruption. When she came to a stop, he said, "Margaret, this is a pretty wild story you're telling me."

"It's true!"

"I can't just round up some men and drive everyone out to the mine on one lttle girl's say-so."

"Why not?"

"Because you're telling me that the most important, most respected man in River Bend is planning to kill George Wilson, in a cave-in, and you're talking about a whole little room lined with gold. Margaret—would you believe me if I told you that story?"

Bud said, "Margaret—is there anything else you can tell him to help him believe you? I mean—he's right. He's got to have proof. You've got to have something solid to move on someone like Mr. Sharpe, or call out a whole police force to look for a kid."

Wade nodded agreement. "I can't take that responsibility, myself. If I accuse him on the word of a minor he just had a run-in with and can't make it stick, he's going to see me fired. Some people might think you were trying to get even with Mr. Sharpe for embarrassing you like he did. It isn't like that, is it, Margaret?"

"Call Charlie," Margaret pleaded. "He'll believe me."

"He's on his way back now."

Margaret covered her face with her hands. What could she do to make Wade believe? Time was ticking by. George could be getting killed, this minute, if he wasn't dead already.

Then, she remembered the nugget, and the diary, in the big willow—and Ruby, who knew the whole story of the nugget from the beginning. "Wade," she said, "let Bud go home and get my diary, and you send someone out for Ruby Dawson. She can tell you whether or not I lied, can't she?"

Wade just sat there.

"Well," Margaret insisted, "if she didn't see my nugget, or test it for me, then you'll know I'm lying. But if she did, then I'm telling you the truth, aren't I?"

Wade studied her for a minute. "O.K.," he said. "I'll send Bud for the diary—and Billy Woodrow for Ruby." He pushed a button on his desk and Billy showed up in the doorway. "But, Margaret, this had better be true. All of it. If you're making this up, and I end up getting fired, you're going to be in big trouble, too. *Big* trouble."

"Hurry, Bud," Margaret begged. "George'll be dead, if we don't hurry. The diary's in the biggest willow on the bank back of the hayfield, in a big hole in the trunk, about four feet up. And the nugget's under the diary."

Bud took off.

Wade said, "Billy, you go pick up Ruby Dawson. Tell her we need her down here for a minute, to help us out."

Billy said, "Smoky Gap Road, right?"

"Right. Go south about a mile out of town. A little shack on the side of a hill . . . right side of the road."

"Got it," Billy said, and left.

"Now," Wade said, grimly, "we wait."

·17·

Margaret could hear Ruby coming. "Get your hands off me, copper!"

"I'm sorry, ma'am. I was just trying to help. I thought you were going to fall."

Ruby came around the corner. "It's these darn boots. Got 'em at a rummage sale. They're too big. Tried soaking them, and everything." She glanced at Margaret. "Well, you're a sight for sore eyes, aren't you?"

"Tell him, Ruby—quickly. Tell him about the nugget!"

Ruby said, "The kid brought me a nugget—and asked me, was it gold?—and I checked it out, and it sure as shootin' was gold—the best I've seen in a coon's age. And she says, 'Well, Mr. Sharpe at the bank was wrong, then, because he said it wasn't.' " She turned to Margaret. "That quick enough for you?"

Margaret pulled at Wade. "You see? I was telling you the truth. Let's go."

Wade said, "Just hold on a minute, here . . . I think Bud's coming."

Bud skidded around the corner and into the office, and tossed Margaret's diary to Wade. "There *was* a little nugget in there, too. Here it is." He laid the nugget on the desk.

Wade opened the diary and bent close to a page near the end.

Bud looked at Margaret. "How are you holding up, Maggie?"

"O.K. If we could just get out to the mine!"

"Connie'll be down later. I'm supposed to look after you till she gets here."

She's coming—to the station?"

"Yup. She had a phone call to make, first. She caught me when I came back from the riverbank. She was waiting beside the car for me, and she had to know what was going on. I told her—and she said, 'I have a very important call to make, but then I'll be right down.' "

"Oh," Margaret said. "She's probably calling Dad." Margaret could imagine the conversation . . . Connie's end, at least. She didn't even want to try to imagine her father's reaction when he learned how she, Margaret, had kept things going smoothly for Connie. This would probably ruin what was left of the relationship between her father and herself. Margaret groaned and put her hands over her ears.

When she looked up again, Charlie Coffey had come back and was walking into the office. Wade took about half a minute to fill him in. Charlie nodded, slipped the diary and the nugget into his desk drawer, and locked the drawer carefully. He said, "O.K., Billy—you stay here and cover the desk. Wade, Bud—you come. Margaret, we'll need you."

Ruby said, "I'm coming. I know that country like you know this station."

Charlie nodded. "Wade, call Bob Smith and tell him and his brother we need them up there. You can go by and pick them up. Tell them they're still deputized from the last time they helped us. Go in from Piney Creek. They'll have to break in. Tell them to go real easy. I sure don't want any of us getting caught in a cave-in."

Ruby and Margaret climbed into the back of the cruiser.

"Say—this is twice today, for me," Ruby said. She leaned over the front seat. "Turn on that siren, Charlie."

Charlie said, "No need to call attention, Ruby."

Ruby sat back. "Billy Woodrow put it on for me—all the way down."

"Well, Billy's afraid of you, Ruby—and I'm not."

♦   ♦   ♦

The woods and meadows of the township skimmed by the windows, but still Margaret couldn't help urging Charlie to go faster. "Please, Charlie—George is all alone in there with that crazy Mr. Sharpe."

"Margaret—I'm flying, now!"

When they got near the ridge, Charlie cut off the road and bucketed across open country, getting as close to the cave entrance as he could without gutting the cruiser.

Then they all piled out, and Margaret took the lead over the top of the ridge and down to the cave. Ruby was right behind her all the way, cursing her boots constantly. Charlie and Bud were pressed to keep up.

"Come on," Margaret said. "Hurry up!"

Once inside the mine, Margaret moved as if she were in a trance—concentrating on recognizing one dark stone wall from another, one tunnel opening from all the rest, listening for telltale sounds, watching for any glimmer of light. It was a great relief to reach the place where she hoped Gray would be and actually see him in her flashlight beam. He raised his head and whimpered.

"Poor Gray," Margaret said, kneeling beside him. "Hold on, boy." She looked up. "That's the little gold room I told you about. Mr. Sharpe called it a 'vug'—and there's where Mr. Sharpe shot at George's head. Or almost."

Charlie played his flashlight inside the vug and whistled. The others crowded around Margaret and Gray, peering in over Charlie's shoulders.

Ruby said, "It's all clear to me, now."

Charlie said, "What's that mean, Ruby?"

She shook her head. "Just two and two adding up to four, Charlie, my boy. Before your time. You'll see."

Margaret stood up. "We've got to find George quick." She hated to walk away from Gray again and leave him lying there in pain. How could he possibly understand her doing that? But she had to. Time could be running out for George.

She found the cave-in, at last. It seemed to her that it had taken hours, but Charlie said, "Only about ten minutes, Margaret." They all set to work clearing a hole in the slide so they could crawl through. The thought kept coming back to Margaret that George had actually attacked Mr. Sharpe to save her. If the cave-in had caught and killed George, she didn't think she could bear that. Her hands trembled so she could hardly pick up rocks, and she felt faint and sick to her stomach.

It took a long time—another ten minutes, at least.

They had to work so slowly and carefully in case they started another slide. Margaret felt as if she were trapped in a nightmare . . . one of those dreams where something horrible was bearing down on you, and you struggled to get free and run away, but your feet were stuck in something like molasses or cement. You could only move in a very slow motion or maybe you couldn't move at all. You woke up, finally, screaming . . . or crying.

Charlie went through the opening first, with his pistol drawn. Margaret called, "Is there anybody there, Charlie?" and her voice was quavery. She cleared her throat. "George isn't over there—is he, Charlie?"

It seemed like a long time before Charlie answered. Then, he said, "No. George isn't here, Margaret. No sign of either of them."

Margaret sagged with relief. She hadn't killed him in the cave-in. It was funny, sort of, how relieved she was that she hadn't done anything to Mr. Sharpe, either.

When she climbed through to the other side, Charlie said, "Our best bet, now, is to let George know we're here . . . in case he's hiding somewhere."

"But Mr. Sharpe will hear us, too," Margaret said.

"More than likely. But we can't help that. I'll carry the only light. The rest of you—lights out. And if anything happens, Bud—you get everyone back to the Smith brothers and Wade, on the Piney Creek side of this place. Head down. That way."

Bud said, "Yes, sir!" All the lights but Charlie's went out, and the darkness came in closer.

Margaret was the first one to call—lightly, so as not to start another cave-in. "George? George! It's me, Margaret. Are you there?"

Nobody answered.

·18·

Ruby said, "These skinny little tracks are like Main Street in a mine, so let's follow them."

Charlie said, "Right." He called again, in a hoarse whisper. "George! George Wilson. This is Charlie Coffey. We're here to get you out. Can you hear me?"

Everyone stopped and waited. Nothing. The group started moving again, talking in very low tones, bumping into each other, tripping over bits of rock every so often. A tiny shuffling noise, behind her, caught Margaret's attention. There it was again. She slowed down and let the others pass, and then followed along, in the rear. What was that noise? Not a rat. Not water dripping. The skin on her arms rose in goose bumps, and she shivered. Her ears felt as if they were going up into points, she was listening so hard. She kept on moving but she said nothing.

Now—there it was again—maybe twenty or thirty feet

back. It was hard to judge distances, in the mine.

She leaned forward over Ruby's shoulder. "Did you hear something, just then?"

Ruby said, "It's a rat, honey—or maybe the mine settling a little."

Margaret shook her head. A chill ran over her. She said, "I think I've heard something like that before."

Charlie stopped and played his flashlight on the floor. They were at an intersection of tunnels.

Ruby moved up to a spot beside Charlie. "Keep following the tracks," she said. "They should take us out to Wade or out to the Long Branch side, and maybe George Wilson has figured that out, too."

Margaret let them go on ahead and stepped into the opening of the tunnel on her right. She waited, quietly. Now they were maybe twenty feet ahead of her. She could still see the wide, warm glow from Charlie's flashlight, and hear the murmur of their voices.

And then—just as she had feared—there was the sound of a footstep, so close it could have been one of her own. Margaret almost screamed, but she managed to hold it in. Someone stepped between her and the light up ahead . . . someone crouching down, stalking the rescue party. In silhouette, against Charlie's light, she could see him raising a gun. Mr. Sharpe! And he was going to shoot!

Margaret threw her flashlight right at Mr. Sharpe's back and yelled, "Charlie! Look out! Behind you!" The flashlight clattered across the stone floor.

Mr. Sharpe cursed, Margaret ducked back into her tunnel, and Charlie yelled, "Everyone down!"—all in a second or two. Then, a gun went off twice—or two guns went off once each. From the ceiling of the tunnel, loose dust and rock began to fall, and Margaret squatted down, terrified, waiting for an avalanche of boulders to bury her.

Ruby, in the tunnel ahead, swore out loud. There was a dull thud, and a groan. Then, silence. Margaret took a deep breath. Well, at least they were not all going to be buried alive.

She peeked around the tunnel corner. Charlie was still standing, holding his flashlight and his gun on Mr. Sharpe, who was sprawled on top of Ruby, who was lying on the tunnel floor. In the darkness, Mr. Sharpe must have thought he was being attacked from the rear and bolted down the tunnel, coming to a quick stop when he ran into Ruby.

Charlie called, "Margaret? You O.K.?"

"I'm O.K."

"Good move, Margaret."

"Thank you, Charlie."

Charlie hauled Mr. Sharpe to his feet. "Have you done anything to George Wilson? Do you know where he is?"

Mr. Sharpe shook his head. "The boy got away. There was a cave-in. It knocked me down—knocked me out a moment, I think."

Charlie said, "You have no idea where he is?"

"No."

Ruby picked herself up, brushing off Bud's offer of assistance. "When did you find this vug, Sam?"

"Ten years ago." Margaret could hardly hear him.

"What'd you do to Edward?" Ruby asked. "Did you kill him?"

Mr. Sharpe looked at her. "You can see how it was for me," he said, as if he was begging her to understand. "I'd studied gold. I appreciated it. I knew what the vug was— how wonderful it was. He would have just pulled all the gold out and left an empty hole. All he ever cared about was enjoying himself. He'd have spent it on trash in a year. He had no appreciation. He didn't deserve it, the way I did."

He looked at Charlie as if he were explaining something very simple to him. "I took care of it—the vug. I came up here every night and looked at it."

Margaret said, "It was you? . . . coming up the riverbank that night?"

He turned on her. "This was your fault," he snarled. "You caused this. When you kept poking around, looking for gold, I knew you'd push your way in here, sooner or later. I knew it was you, under the trees. I could see where you'd run home. Oh, yes. I had to watch *you* all the time, after that—and try to find out what you knew and if you were telling anyone else. Every night I had to watch out for *you*! I tried to warn you—to stay away from the mine—didn't I? But you wouldn't listen. You wouldn't stop."

"This is where you took Bozo every night?" Margaret asked.

Mr. Sharpe shook his head. He looked down at the floor of the tunnel, and his voice dropped again. "Bozo was Edward's dog. He . . . he kept on looking for Edward in the mine, after . . . you know how some dogs are." He shuddered. "I couldn't stop him. So I had to keep him tied up in case he ever came back up here and started digging."

He paused. "I thought maybe I ought to . . . to do away with him." He spread his hands down and out in a final gesture, and he sighed. "But then I would have had no one . . . no one," he said. "And then I saw how I could say I was walking him every night and come up here, instead—and no one would ever ask any questions if I was just walking my dog."

"Is Edward in here, Mr. Sharpe?" Charlie asked, quietly.

"Yes."

"Where?"

"One of the dead ends, in the oldest part of the mine. I buried him down there."

They were all silent for a minute. Margaret felt sick, and her knees started to shake, and she had to sit down suddenly. That dog howling every night, downriver— that had been poor old Bozo. Tied up and waiting, while Mr. Sharpe went up to the mine—up the river, past her house.

Charlie said, "I'm going to take Mr. Sharpe out to the cruiser and handcuff him there. I'll be back as soon as I can, to help look for George. If you find him first, head out toward the Piney Creek entrance."

◆   ◆   ◆

Bud and Margaret and Ruby walked on down the tunnel, pausing, every so often, to call—softly—and to listen. "If he can still answer us, he's not anywhere around here," Bud said. "That's for sure."

"Well, he's somewhere—and we're going to find him. I'm not leaving this mine till we do. And we've got to go back for poor Gray, too."

She stopped dead in her tracks. Gray! Of course! That was the answer. George would be worrying about Gray too, and be trying to work his way back to his dog.

"If George is all right, if Mr. Sharpe didn't get him, then he'll find Gray," Margaret said, and turned around. "So that's where I'm going—back to Gray."

"Can you even find him? I've turned around so often already, I don't know where I'm at," Bud said.

"I can sure try."

Bud looked at the crumbling ceiling over their heads.

"Make it fast, Margaret. This whole mine could collapse like a wet paper bag. I don't want to be around when it does."

◆　　◆　　◆

"He ought to be near here," Margaret said, a few minutes later, "unless I missed a turn." They were in a much smaller tunnel, now, cut out of rock. It was beginning to look familiar.

"Call again," Bud said, "but easy—real easy."

"George?" Margaret called. "Can you hear me?"

And, from around a bend in the tunnel, came back an answer. Faintly. "Over here. We've been wondering when you would remember us."

◆　　◆　　◆

It took sending out to the cruiser for tools and about half an hour of difficult, delicate work to get Gray out of the trap without hurting him to any greater degree—but Charlie, Bud, and Ruby did it. George stayed by his head and talked to him the whole while.

"Clean break," Charlie said, at last. "He'll mend."

Bud and George picked Gray up very carefully and headed out of the mine. Ruby walked behind them, telling them what they were doing wrong, every step of the way.

Margaret leaned into the vug after they left and touched some of the gold glittering on its floor. "Charlie?"

"Margaret?"

"You know that I lost my father's nugget. That's what started all this, because I didn't want to have to tell him. Could I take a nugget—just one—so I will have something to give back to him?"

"Technically speaking, we're not supposed to hand out samples of the state's evidence. Besides"—Charlie leaned over her shoulder and played his flashlight around the inside of the vug—"I don't see anything here that looks like your dad's nugget. That came down the branch, I expect . . . bouncing along the bottom and getting all rounded and smoothed. This stuff is more like flakes. And white and gold crystals."

Margaret could feel her eyes getting hot in back, as if she were going to cry. She blinked hard. "He is going to be awfully disappointed in me. And that nugget I found is so much smaller than his."

Charlie rubbed his chin. "Well, if it hadn't been for you, I'd be long gone, by now—and that goes for George Wilson, too, most likely. So you just help yourself to a couple of those bigger flakes—the ones like my thumbnail—and give them to your dad. He can see about having them made into something for his key chain. Gold's soft and real easy to work. Maybe they can make him up a big gold C—for Cassidy. That would look real nice, wouldn't it?"

"Thank you, Charlie."

"Thank you, Miss Cassidy."

Margaret reached into the little gleaming room and picked up several gold flakes. They glowed in her hand like golden fish scales—but she didn't care for gold any more. When she thought what it had almost cost her and everyone else—when she thought about poor Bozo, and Edward who hadn't drowned at all but was buried in the mine—she didn't care if she ever saw it, or wore it, again. She looked back into the vug. It was really a trap . . . a golden trap. It had already killed Edward and it had ruined Sam Sharpe forever—and it had hurt poor Gray, and almost caused her and George to be killed. She turned away from it.

Wade and the Smith brothers arrived and stood in the

entrance to the vug, hardly able to believe what they were seeing. But Margaret went and sat down with her back up against the tunnel wall, waiting for her legs to stop feeling like overcooked spaghetti.

When they got to the station, the first thing that everyone noticed was a two-tone, silvery gray Cadillac parked in Charlie's space.

Ruby and Bud said "Wow!" in chorus.

Charlie said, "It must be the regional inspector. What form did I forget to fill out now?"

Just inside the station door, Connie was waiting. A tall, gray-haired man stood beside her. He was wearing a gray, pin-striped suit, and his briefcase looked as if it was made out of real leather.

Connie said, "Margaret, honey—are you all right?"

Margaret nodded. "And George is O.K., too—and so is Gray."

"Oh, that's wonderful. I am so relieved." She turned to Charlie. "This gentleman is Judson Wolfe. He is a lawyer, from Caswell Corners, and if Margaret is still in any kind of trouble, Judson will be representing her from now on."

Charlie held out his hand. "How about that! Judson Wolfe. I've heard about you, Mr. Wolfe, but I never expected to see you in River Bend."

Mr. Wolfe smiled. "Mrs. Cassidy is an old friend of mine—and when she heard that her stepdaughter might need help, she asked me to come to River Bend. She can be very insistent."

"Then you were calling Mr. Wolfe, when Bud left," Margaret said, "not Dad?"

"Why would I call your father? He's two thousand miles away," Connie said. "If you needed help, it was my job . . . that's what I always wanted to do . . . just to help.

Before he left, your father said, 'Take care of Dempsey . . . she's mighty important to me.' And I'm—"

Margaret interrupted. "He said that? He really said that?"

"Yes, he did. And you haven't given me many chances to take care of you. I blame myself for letting you struggle through this, all alone. But every time I tried to get close to you—every time you were angry, or unhappy, or worried—and I hoped you'd sit down and talk to me about it, you would walk off, or close up."

"But they told me not to bother you . . . not to worry or upset you."

"Who told you that?" Connie demanded. "Not me. Listen, Margaret—I can take worry. I can take bother. And not too much upsets me. But it's hard, being shut out. I thought it was that you didn't like me—or didn't trust me—and I could understand that. I *am* a stepmother—and you people had everything worked out the way you wanted it, and were doing fine, till I showed up. But it hurts."

"We should have leveled with each other, no matter what everyone else said," Margaret said.

"Well, there's no time like the present," Connie said briskly, and took a deep breath. "Margaret—you go into that mine just one more time, and I'm going to put you on bread and water for a solid week."

Margaret laughed.

◆　　◆　　◆

It was almost time for school to start again. Mr. Sharpe's hearing had been held, and he had been sent away to a special kind of prison for people who were not mentally responsible. Charlie called Margaret down to his office, late one afternoon, and gave her back her diary.

Margaret didn't go into the house, when she got home. She wanted to think, so she went down to the riverbank.

Someone who didn't even live in River Bend was going to inherit the mine. No one knew what they'd do with it—and Margaret didn't care. She was never going back in that mine again.

Things had changed, at home. The Cassidy house was a noisier place, now. People talked about the things that bothered them—and sometimes, they actually shouted at each other, and that was all right, too. When someone was sad, they weren't ashamed to cry, and let other people know. And with all the talking, and shouting, and crying that had been let out, came more laughing, too. Margaret nodded. Everyone was happier, now—except maybe Lilian, who had to do the dishes a third of the time, and pay real money for baby-sitting when she'd said she would, and treat Margaret like a regular person.

Margaret opened the diary. The last entry was for the day after the flash flood, almost two months ago. Two months! She couldn't believe it had been that long—but when you could say what you felt, you didn't need to write it down, and hide it.

She remembered a poem Connie had read to her.

> At a little pond in the woods
> I decided: this is the center of my life.
> I threw a big stick far out, to be
> all the burdens from earlier years.
> Ever since, I have been walking
> lightly, looking around, out of the woods.

◆　　◆　　◆

The sun was setting behind the trees. The river was making soft, contented sounds as it flowed past, well within its bed. Margaret walked to the edge of the water, threw her diary into the river, and watched it sink. Then she turned and walked lightly out from under the willows.